DOUBLE WOW

DOUBLE WOW

Shellie Green-Baker

Library of Congress Control Number:		2018902390
ISBN:	Hardcover	978-1-9845-0935-2
	Softcover	978-1-9845-0936-9
	eBook	978-1-9845-0937-6

Print information available on the last page.

Rev. date: 02/21/2018

To order additional copies of this book, contact:
Xlibris
1-888-795-4274
www.Xlibris.com
Orders@Xlibris.com
774087

CHAPTER ONE

Chad stood and watched the three young riders head in for supper. They were all laughing at the little prank they had just pulled off.

"She'll be madder than a wounded bear by the time she gets back here," Chad heard the oldest rider say.

"Ya, and I don't aim to be 'round when she gets back neither," the youngest chuckled.

Chad watched as the young men tied off their mounts and started off for the house. "You men will eat after you take care of those horses and not a minute sooner," he hollered out to them.

"Ah, Chad, we need some grub. We be starvin'," this came from the oldest of the group, James, who was fifteen. Next to him stood his two younger brothers. They were the youngest set of twins, Tom and Tim, who were thirteen. All three boys had their hands on their hips, trying to defy Chad.

"Not a minute sooner." Chad's voice had his authority tone to it, so the matter was dropped as the young men turned back to their horses, grumbling all the way.

Chad stood there, shaking his head with a grin across his face. He had been with the Holt family for four years now. When he came to work for them, he had been twenty-five. In that four years' time, he had become very attached to every one of them. They were as close as a family could get and not be blood related.

Chad stood six feet three inches tall, with wavy blond hair. His build was like a brick from all the hard work that comes with running a five-hundred-acre-plus ranch in Rescue, California. Chad was on the quiet side. He minded his own business most of the time. He didn't like butting in too much, but he found that as the boys got older, he had to be more of an authoritative figure.

Now that the boys were taking care of their horses, Chad decided to go wash up in his separate quarters of the bunkhouse.

Twenty minutes later, Chad came around the corner of the main house and heard a shouting match going on. It seemed he was going to have to intervene again. His heart went out to Mr. Charles Holt's wife, Evelyn. Since her husband's death three months earlier, she was running into all kinds of heartache from her boys.

She turned to Chad at her wit's end. "Chad, they done it again." The strain in her voice was evident.

"What's that, ma'am?"

"Those boys are up to their tricks again. They gone and dropped off Katrina out by the ole watering hole." The frustration and strain showed in her eyes. Chad couldn't help but feel a bit of her frustration. On the other hand, he couldn't help but chuckle either. He knew Katrina could take care of herself, and now it was clear—the snickering as the young men rode in a bit ago was at Katrina's expense. It seemed they were always pulling pranks on each other, and Katrina was just as good, if not better than the boys, in dishing it out.

"What ya find so funny, Chad?" Evelyn snapped. "She ain't got a horse or pistol with her. This time, things have gone too far."

Chad's face fell with this bit of information. As a matter of fact, he was beginning to scowl. It was one thing to leave her out there as a joke, but to leave her totally defenseless was altogether another matter.

"Why those . . ." Chad ground out.

Evelyn thought quickly while pushing and shooing the boys inside the house with one hand as she was holding Chad off with the other.

"I'll let you tear into those boys' hides when ya get back. Just get out there and bring her home"—her voice started to crack—"before a rattler gets her or . . ." She couldn't finish, and Chad knew just what she was thinking.

Three months ago, he was the one to ride up on Charles Holt, who was lying facedown in the dirt, with an arrow at the back of his skull. Chad shuddered at the memory. He looked down to see Mrs. Holt holding back a sob.

Before she could remember any more of that nightmare, Chad spoke up. "I'll find her, ma'am. She's fine. No one would have the guts to go near her. She's too mean."

He was trying to lift her spirits, and she knew it. Chad had been such a rock since her husband's death, and to be honest, if he hadn't taken charge of everything, and she meant everything, she didn't know what would have become of the ranch. With Chad there, she didn't have to worry about too much, but this was something he had no control over. She just hoped he could get to Katrina before it was too late. With a heavy sigh, she said, "Thanks, Chad."

He was just turning to leave when the screen door opened. "Chad, I'll go with you," James spoke up.

"I think you've done enough."

"Well, she deserved it."

Chad had a flashback of the morning before. He had seen the sparkle in Katrina's eyes when she headed for the barn yesterday, struggling with two buckets of water. He had asked her if he could give her a hand, and she had told him this was up to her. He just figured she was giving the horses some water and went back to work.

Ten minutes later, Chad witnessed that as James came out the left barn door, the bucket of water that had been resting on the ledge came pouring down on James's head, and if that wasn't enough, the bucket hit him so hard he went down on his knees.

Chad had to admit that his gut ached from laughing so hard, and he literally had tears in his eyes when Tom walked through the right barn door and was also soaked. She'd gotten them both back in one act. Chad remembered thinking, *She would have to pay for that one.*

"Look, James, the jokes are good and well. We all never have a dull moment around here because of you and your siblings, but when it turns to someone being put in danger, the fun is over. You not only left Katrina without a horse but you also took her gun, and in case you haven't noticed, it's getting dark."

James started to realize the danger that was his fault. "I'm sorry, Chad, Mom. I guess we just didn't think."

Chad turned to Evelyn. "I'll be back." Then he turned to James. "If I were you, I'd find a safe place to hide." He headed down the steps. "Better take Tom and Tim with you. Katrina won't let this one slide. She will have your hide."

Chad mounted his horse and headed out. The sun was already setting. If he knew Katrina, and he thought he knew her pretty well, she would be spitting nails. He had to smile. Katrina was like no other nineteen-year-old woman he had ever met. And yes, at nineteen, she had to be called a woman, but you wouldn't know it from a distance. She was built small all over. She barely reached five feet. She wore the boys' jeans all the time, along with their shirts. She never wore her hair down and kept it pulled up in a hat all the time. Chad couldn't remember the last time he had seen it down. He couldn't even tell how long it was. Yes, from a distance, she looked like a boy. But up close was another matter altogether. She was too damn pretty to be a boy.

Chad noticed the sun going behind the hills. The ole watering hole was a good half hour on horseback at a good pace. "Come on, Streak, let's get to her in record time." Chad spurred Streak on.

Katrina sat and watched her brothers ride off with her horse and gun. They were all laughing at what they were going to get away with. She laughed too; she deserved this one. The only drawback she saw was that she was starving. They had all skipped lunch to round up a few calves that had strayed. She watched as her three younger brothers rode out of sight.

Katrina got up from where they had dumped her and brushed off the dust. She filled her canteen from the watering hole and took a huge drink, hoping it would fill the void.

She laughed again then slapped her hat on her head, tucking her hair up inside, and started to put one foot in front of the other to get home.

It wasn't bad for an August afternoon; it was actually pretty mild, weather-wise. Katrina loved this country. The range went on for as far as you could see. The sky was clear. She knew the sun would be going down before she got home, so she picked up her pace. She figured she would be home in about three hours if she were lucky.

Katrina was deep in thought but not deep enough to not hear the *snap*. She stopped dead in her tracks. She slowly looked around. There was nothing that she could see and no more noise, so she went on but kept very alert. She scolded herself for taking this so lightly; it really wasn't safe for her to be out here without her gun. "When I get home," she cursed her brothers.

When she heard another twig snap, the hairs at the back of her neck stood up. She started to laugh. "Okay, you guys, I knew you would not leave me out here alone. Come on out." She expected one of them to jump out at her. No one did. This was getting scary. She didn't like not having her gun. It could just be a deer. The sun was starting to go down, and they liked to feed at dusk.

Nevertheless, Katrina's pace was picking up; she wasn't enjoying this prank anymore.

There was a *thud*. "Oof!" Katrina had been attacked from the back. She was eating dirt and trying to spit it out. "Get off me, you jerk." She thought it was one of her brothers.

Katrina was rolled over abruptly and was looking at the face of an Indian. He looked at her closely, his eyes squinting at her as if he was questioning her. Then he started undoing her shirt with swift fingers. Katrina began slapping and hitting him. "Get your hands off me."

That didn't stop him; he didn't stop until he had her unveiled. Then he grabbed her hat and pulled it off. Beautiful thick blonde hair fell out all over. "What? Seeing my breasts bound was not enough proof I am a girl? You idiot, get off me."

Katrina could see the shock on his face. He obviously had thought she was a boy. She was still struggling to get free of him, especially now that he knew she was a girl. He might try to rape her. His expression changed, and she thought he was going to do just that. "Not on your life." She spat and began to kick and push. Just when she was loose enough, she tried covering herself, but he yanked so hard on her shirt he pulled one of the sleeves off.

"Hey! What are you doing? That is a new shirt." Her words were for naught as he roughly pulled her to him and tied her hands behind her back with her shirtsleeve. "What are you doing? Stop!" Nothing was getting to him.

He had to push her hair out of the way as he was tying her hands together. He had never in his life seen so much hair. The color was also striking. It glowed in the sun, and because it had a natural wave, it picked up the red as the sun started to set. It didn't look real, so he ran his hands through it. Katrina yanked away.

As he hoisted her up on his horse, she continued to kick him. He thought she didn't weigh much more than his wolf. When she started to protest and fight him again, he decided he liked her spirit. What he was going to do with her, he didn't know.

What he did next surprised Katrina. With swift fingers, he buttoned her shirt. Then he straddled the horse behind her and put a death grip around her waist.

Katrina didn't like this one bit. "Where are you taking me? You cannot just ride off into the sunset with me." There was no answer. "Ew, just wait till I get my hands on you, James," she fumed. "Look, let's be sensible here. Just let me go, and no one has to know about our little meeting." There was still no response.

As they rode on, Katrina began to have this overwhelming fear sweep over her. Then she realized that she had never felt fear like this before. She was his prisoner, and at the moment, she had nothing to help her. She could not believe this was happening to her.

They rode on for what seemed like hours. He was having second thoughts about taking her with him. He had only one use for a woman, and it had been a long time. And she had spunk, so the fight would be worth it, but his day didn't start out with the plan to kidnap a white woman.

As they rode, her hands became very bothersome. With them tied behind her back and her seated in front of him, they were cradled in his crotch. He shifted a couple of times, but it was of no use. He was going to have to rearrange things, or he would no doubt become *very* uncomfortable.

Katrina felt him squirming behind her. She was mortified when she realized what his problem was. She tried not to move her hands at all, but they were getting cramped and the sleeve he had tied her with was cutting off her circulation.

She spoke up. "I know you do not understand what I am saying, but if you could just loosen up the ties on my wrist, I would appreciate it. My fingers are going numb." She moved her fingers as little as possible at this point and looked down behind her so he would get the idea. He just pulled her tighter up against him. She could feel him growing against her hands; she couldn't believe it. This was not a good sign.

Of course, he was reacting to her like this. He hadn't been with a woman for two years. They were nothing but trouble. It was because of a woman that he left his tribe two years ago, only visiting if necessary. He was going to allow himself to be aroused, take this woman, and be done with her.

Fortunately, five minutes later, they were at the spot where he had been camping for the last two days. His wolf ran up to greet them. He told the wolf in his language, "Good boy, we have a guest."

Katrina saw the wolf approach them and heard the softness in his voice. He couldn't really be talking to the wolf, as if he was a pet, could he? She looked around and saw he had a small camp that the wolf had been guarding.

"Nice place you have here," she exclaimed, as he took her down from the horse. "But I do not think I will be staying. So if you will just untie me, we will just pretend this never happened." She waited a few minutes to see if she would have any response from him.

It had been dark for over an hour, but with hands untied or not, she was determined to leave. After all, the moon was full, and she could find her way home. She had lived in this country all her life; it wouldn't be that hard.

Feeling very uneasy, she spoke up, "It has been nice knowing you, but I really need to get home. My family will be worried about me." With that said, she started to walk away from camp.

She didn't get too far. Silver Ghost grabbed her arm and turned her around. In his language, he said, "You stay with me tonight!"

Something in his voice told her she should be afraid. He guided her back to the camp. As he bent to start a fire, Katrina made a run for it. She scurried as fast as she could to climb up the rock and jumped onto the back of his horse. With a swift kick, she yelled, "Ya!" Unfortunately, his wits were too good because the horse hadn't even moved a foot from the rock, and he had jumped on behind her, turning the horse around.

Katrina had a few choice words she wanted to spit out. He was going to get an earful, but she was so angry at the moment she couldn't even speak. What made her angrier was she felt tears well up in her eyes, and she never cried, not easily anyway.

"Damn you." She breathed heavily and jerked from him. "You are not going to be that easy to get away from, are you?"

He almost laughed but kept it under control. He put her down on the ground and walked over to his belongings. Katrina got as good a look at him as she could in the full moon. He seemed very tall with a strong build. He's too strong for her to take on. His hair was straight, and under the moon, it looked blue. It was shoulder-length, and two small braids were at his temples.

As he approached Katrina, he held out a bundle to her. She couldn't take it with her hands tied. "Oh, something for me. You should not have. No problem. Just let me take that with my teeth," she sarcastically scolded him. Silver Ghost wanted to burst out laughing at her sharp tongue, but he hid his humor.

Silver Ghost just dropped the bundle in her lap. He then started to undo the buttons of her blouse again.

"Oh no, you are not." Katrina jerked away from him. Next, he pulled a knife from his waistband. The alarm was evident on her face. "What are you going to do with that? Slit my throat?"

Silver Ghost turned her around really fast and cut the bindings from her wrist. She started rubbing and stretching her wrists and fingers. She felt the burning sensation of blood flowing.

He picked the bundle up from her lap and pushed it toward her chest.

"What? You want me to open this?" She laid it out on her lap and untied the package. Then she exploded. "No way, Mr . . . Mr . . . whatever your name is. You are not getting me to put this thing on. I am not accustomed to wearing dresses, let alone something so small." She sat there for a second and just started to shake her head. "What am I doing? You do not even understand a word I am saying."

Silver Ghost turned around so she wouldn't see his smile and proceeded to stoke the fire. He could feel her staring at his back, and he wasn't letting her out of sight. She was just sizing him up, and there was no contest.

As he built the fire, he had a flashback on when he first tackled her. He was so shocked to find she was a girl. Girl, hell, she was a woman. By the size of her breast that she kept bound so well, he would guess she wasn't a teenager. And why did she dress in boy's clothes and bind herself? She was a peculiar one, but what had him so intrigued was her hair. It fell all the way to her knees with a natural wave, and the way the moon caught it, it glowed. He couldn't wait to run his fingers through it again.

So far, he couldn't tell what the rest of her looked like because of all those boys' clothes, but all would be told when she put the dress on.

Katrina stood there with her hands on her hips. There was no way she was going to change, not until she saw the look in his eyes that told her he wouldn't take no for an answer. "All right, all right, I will change, you miserable brute. I suppose you think I would give you the pleasure of changing me? I will tell you something though, I will not change in front of you." She stepped behind his horse.

He went back to stirring the fire. Out of the corner of his eye, he could see her shirt hit the ground then her pants. He was starting to feel his own fire start to stir. He would take her after dinner.

A few minutes later, Katrina stepped out from behind the horse. She was tugging at the material, trying to stretch it. This dress was way too tight and didn't even cover her knees. She looked up and immediately felt embarrassed. "This thing is way too small. Could I please put my clothes back on? You cannot seriously expect me to wear this!"

He just stared. He would never have believed that that entire woman was wrapped up in those boys' clothes. He was itching to have her right then and there. What to do with her after is what was bothering him.

She croaked, "What are you staring at?" His eyes hadn't left her, and she had no idea what she looked like. She just knew she needed to get away from him soon because he had a look in his eyes that was really scaring her.

She crossed her arms over her chest. She hated his eyes on her. She knew she was developing way too much for her taste, and that was one of the main reasons she kept herself bound all the time. She had no use for any man's attentions.

There had only been one crush she could ever remember having, and that was for Chad, who never even paid any attention to her. He thought he was too old for her.

"STOP IT!" she shouted. She couldn't stand his staring anymore.

This brought him back to reality. He literally had to shake himself to snap out of the trance she had put him in. He stood up, and as soon as he did, Katrina took off running.

He was quick in pursuit, right on her heels. Tackling her from behind, she slammed into the ground face-first *again*.

"Get off me," she demanded.

He abruptly rolled her over, and before she could say any more, he kissed her full on the mouth. Katrina had only been kissed by a man once before, and that was when Chad gave her a peck on the cheek at her last birthday party. That kiss had meant the world to her.

This kiss was scaring her to death. She was fighting him to get off but couldn't even budge him an inch.

She was a wildcat and very inexperienced in kissing, and as much as he was enjoying her fight, here in the dirt wasn't where he wanted to have her. He got up abruptly and pulled her with him back to camp.

As they were walking back, they both stopped in unison as they heard the rattler. When it struck, she expected to be bit, but the pain never came. Everything happened so fast. The wolf had intervened, and the snake was as good as dead.

He picked it up with a stick and held it in front of Katrina. He was literally shocked when she took it from the stick and sat down by the fire and proceeded to clean it for cooking.

Katrina was so thankful for the interruption. She kept herself busy preparing the snake for dinner. She knew what he had on his mind, and she wanted no part in it. What she was going to do, she had no idea, but she had to think of something fast. Snake didn't take long to cook.

Shortly after, they sat and ate the snake with some berries he had picked. Katrina was getting so tired all of a sudden. It was no wonder with the day she had put in. It had to be at least ten o'clock, which was past her normal bedtime. Living on a cattle ranch, you definitely turned in early and got up early. With her belly full, she couldn't help expelling a huge yawn. Immediately, she was embarrassed when he smiled at her.

"Okay, so I am a little tired. Do you people get tired?" She didn't like the look in his eyes. The last thing she wanted to do was give him the idea she was ready for bed.

He continued to smile at her as he stood up, the look on his face very telling.

Katrina felt fear grip her as he approached her. There was no doubt he thought he was going to kiss her again, not to mention what else he had on his mind.

She put up her hands to block him. "Oh no, do not come any closer!" Katrina yelled at him. "I will kill you before I let you lay a hand on me." Her words sounded empty to her own ears, let alone to someone who didn't understand her language. She didn't think she had a prayer left. In that instant, she knew he was going to rape her because she was in no way going to submit to him.

Just as she was getting ready to scream, just as she thought her luck had run out, just as he pulled her to him, a growl that would make your hair stand on end filled both their ears. Katrina was thrown backward as a mountain lion jumped at the Indian from behind, knocking them both to the ground. The struggling was fierce. Legs, arms, and blood were everywhere. The wolf, mountain lion, and the Indian were fighting to get the upper hand while all on top of her. Katrina could tell the Indian was trying to protect her, and the mountain lion didn't care. It was going to kill them.

She was finally able to get out from under the pile and watch as the mountain lion was tearing him to shreds while his wolf was tearing the mountain lion to shreds. Katrina looked around for a weapon. The only thing she could see was a large boulder. She had to make her aim good and not hit the wolf or else that beast would turn on her. She raised it high and came crashing down as hard as she could. She heard the skull break; blood gushed out. She had done it. The struggle was over. Both man and beast lay completely still. She didn't know if the Indian was still alive or not. His wolf stood back, sizing her up and down.

"What?" she asked the wolf, trying to not be afraid of him.

It took all her strength to roll the mountain lion off him. She groaned. "Are you all right?" There was no answer. She saw his knife in his hand. It had been of no use. She told herself to take it and run. Now she could get away—just take his horse and go. She looked at him lying there with blood all over him. She didn't know if it was his or the mountain lion's. It didn't matter. From what she could see, he was dead. She guessed he saved her life; for that, she was grateful.

She turned to get his horse, and she heard a groan. *Damn, he was still alive.* She had to see him. It wasn't in her to leave a man to die, even if he was just about to rape her a few minutes before. She thought herself nothing but a fool, but when he moaned again, she went to him.

He was trying to say something to her. She lowered herself to his mouth, and he whispered something she couldn't understand.

That was the last he said for several days.

CHAPTER TWO

Chad kept his eyes out for Katrina on the way to the watering hole. He half expected to come across her walking. So far, there was no sign of her.

When he reached the watering hole, he didn't see her anywhere. "Katrina, its Chad. Are you here?" he called this out several times.

He dismounted and walked around a bit. He came across her hat. By the looks of things, there had been a stuggle. He was by no means a scout, but the ground was all messed up, and her hat was ground into the dirt.

The problem was he didn't know if she had fought with the boys to get some leverage on the situation or if there had been some foul play with another person.

"Katrina!" he hollered out again. His gut was telling him something was wrong. He didn't like the feel of this one bit. He needed to ask some questions to the boys, and there wasn't much he could do now that it was getting dark.

He mounted again and hoped against all hope that he somehow missed her on the way out. At the pace he was riding, she could have called out for him and he wouldn't have heard her.

He slapped her hat against his horse's rump and headed back, stopping every now and then along the way to call out her name.

Katrina had been a sweet pain in his side ever since he started working for her parents. She was always in the middle of the pack. She had to be included in everything and was spoiled by her daddy to boot.

Chad always felt a need to keep a close eye out for her, not that she couldn't hold her own most of the time, but she was just a little girl trying to live in a man's world of work.

If anything has happened to her, he would skin those boys alive.

She was nowhere. His only hope was he had missed her somehow and she was already home safe and sound. When he reached the house, he tied his horse and took the steps of the porch, two at a time. He didn't even bother to knock.

"Is she here?" he demanded, but the look on Evelyn's face answered his question.

Chad turned to James and roared, "Did one of you have a struggle with Katrina before you left her out there?"

Bo, Katrina's twin brother, walked in the back door. "Hi, all." He started to say something then stopped when he saw all the glum faces. "What's the matter? Somebody die?"

Bo turned to Chad. "What's wrong?" Bo knew he could depend on Chad to spell it out.

"Your three little brothers pulled a good one on Katrina this afternoon. They left her without her horse or gun out by the ole watering hole. When I got out there, all I found of her was this." Chad held up her rumpled hat.

James, the fifteen-year-old, chimed in. "She's probably pulling a fast one on all of us. She's probably just fine and having a laugh right now, hiding out and making us all sweat and worry about her."

Chad wasn't even going to acknowledge that one. He turned on James again. "I asked you a question. Did any of you have a struggle with her?"

"No," James croaked. None of them had seen Chad this angry before, and they weren't sure how to handle him.

Chad was seeing red. He was worried to death about Katrina but had to hope she was playing another game. With this family, you could never tell.

When he finally spoke up, his voice was raspy. "If anything has happened to her, you boys will answer to me. Do I make myself clear?"

All three boys answered at the same time with their heads down that they understood.

Chad headed for the door. "I'm going to round up a few men and head out at sunup."

The boys all shouted their wanting to help.

"No, thanks. I'm too angry to have you along." Chad slammed the screen door and left.

Bo followed. "Chad, I'll be one of the men that goes along in the morning."

Chad liked Bo. He would have made his pa proud of the hard work he had been putting in on the ranch since his death. "Sunup then," Chad declared.

Bo just nodded. Chad noticed Evelyn standing at the screen door. She looked as white as a sheet.

"I'll find her. I promise." With that, Chad headed for the front bunkhouse, hoping he wouldn't let her down.

The men were all cleaning up their dinner. Chad got their attention just by clearing his throat. "I want three men to ride out with me in the early morning to search for Katrina."

The men started asking questions all at once. The noise level was grating on his nerves. Chad held up his hand to quiet them. He explained the situation. Not one of them was willing to be left behind. They were good men, but he chose carefully of the ones that would be most helpful. He knew for a fact that Bart was a good tracker and was depending on him to lead the way.

Once he picked his three men, Chad turned to go to his room. He saw Bo standing in the doorway. "I'll want to take a packhorse. Let's get some shut-eye."

Bo stopped Chad by touching his arm. "And Katrina's horse. She'll want to have it to ride home on."

Chad knew he couldn't let Bo down either. "Good thinking, Bo. Sunup?" Chad raised his eyebrow in question.

"See you then." Bo headed off to the house, and Chad went to his quarters.

The men were all ready before sunup. They met in the compound where Evelyn had a bundle of food for them to add to their supplies.

"I couldn't sleep last night, so I baked." The nervous fear for her daughter was evident.

Bo walked up to her and gave her a big hug. "Hang in there, Ma. We'll find her."

Those words broke the dam she had been able to hold back until now. "I need her, Bo. She's my only daughter."

Chad had all he could take. If they didn't head out now, he was going to need a hankie himself. "The sooner we get going, the sooner we'll have her home."

Bo pulled away from his mom, and she wiped her eyes. "Don't you come home without her. Do you understand me?" Her question was directed to Chad.

Chad just tipped his hat to her and turned to mount his horse. He couldn't let her down. She had been through enough, and he owed it to her. He would bring her home, or he wouldn't come back.

Chad hadn't gotten any sleep himself last night. He kept expecting to hear the commotion of Katrina's arrival sometime in the night. He kept going over all the memories of her these last couple of years.

He knew she had a crush on him. Who couldn't tell? The men teased him all the time about the looks she gave him and how she was always under his feet asking questions, trying to be helpful. At first, he wanted to deny it, but the last six months had been different. He had grown accustomed to her being in his way. If she wasn't around, he found himself looking for her.

He remembered once when a new hand that had been hired about three months ago inquired about her and how it had rubbed him the wrong way, so he let him go. He had to question himself on that one because he didn't have any feelings other than a brotherly type of protection for her. Then again, she had enough brothers.

As the men rode out to the old watering hole, they combed the area like a fine-toothed comb. Chad didn't want to take a chance. She might be injured and lying unconscious. The area had its share of wolves and mountain lions, not to mention rattlers. If she had tangled with one of them, she could be dead, and he didn't want to think about that. She needed to be okay, for Mrs. Holt's sake.

It had taken them until late afternoon to reach the watering hole, and Chad was frustrated that they had come up with nothing—no sign of her at all, not one little clue.

They were all worn out and hungry, but not one of them had complained that they hadn't taken time to eat. The men were loyal to the Holt family and wanted to find Katrina safe. There wasn't a bush, tree, rock, hill, or stump that hadn't been turned over in the search, and they hadn't found a thing—no clothing, no blood, and no unusual tracks of any sort.

"Look, as much as I hate to admit it, we're all tired, and I'm starting to see cross-eye. We will set up camp here, get some grub and a good night's sleep. We will be fresh in the morning, and hopefully, some kind of clue will show up." Chad would have gone on, but he knew the men needed to rest.

Chad had been right. The following midmorning, Bart, the ranch hand that had experience in tracking, figured that the horse hooves in the dirt weren't all from the ranch. They tracked each one until they found the one that went north instead of south.

They broke camp after an early lunch. The sagebrush made it hard to keep track of the hoofprints. The tracks didn't go in a straight line; they seemed to weave back and forth.

Bart cursed, "This rider was clever as all get-out. The way the tracks keep disappearing, we'll never find her." The discouraging part was they had only traveled about three miles before night had fallen.

"This is where they start up on this side of the creek!" Bo yelled from across the way.

"Good," Chad called back. "We'll set up camp for the night there and start out in the morning."

After supper, Chad took himself for a walk. He felt so worthless. This was taking longer than he had hoped for. If she had been dragged off and was hurt, she could be bleeding to death. The only hope he had to go on was there had been no blood. Hell, he didn't even know if they were even on her tail. This could be a wild-goose chase. They didn't even know if she was on the horse they had been tracking. Just someone passing through could have made these prints. It wasn't uncommon.

"Damn!" She couldn't believe this was happening. "I'll get something to stop the bleeding."

She stood up and walked over to the fire where she could see better. Her shirt still lay on the ground, so she picked it up. It was full of dirt, and the stream they had passed wasn't too far off. She could walk down there and wash the shirt. She looked down at herself; she was also covered with blood. "Man, what did I do to deserve this?"

Katrina grabbed a branch from the fire to light her way to the stream. As she bent, she heard an animal fight on the other side of the boulder. Where was his wolf? She couldn't move. There must have been more than one mountain lion, maybe his mistress. She didn't know for sure, but she ran for the Indian's knife. She wasn't going to be left defenseless again.

The silence was almost too much to bear. Then the wolf came out from behind the boulder, all bloody and limping. When he spotted her with the knife, he began to growl. Katrina had never heard a more eerie sound. She put her hand up to ward the wolf off. "It's okay, boy. I didn't hurt him. I'm going to try to help him and you too if you'll let me.

She slowly backed away from the wolf and headed for the creek. First, she washed the shirt and tore it into strips, and then she washed as much of the blood off her arms and dress without soaking herself. She wasn't sure how cool it would get tonight, and she didn't want to catch a chill.

When she got back to camp, the wolf was lying with his head on the Indian's stomach. Something about the bond pulled at her heart. The wolf lifted his head as she approached. "It's okay, boy. I won't hurt him."

Katrina moved very slowly so as not to startle the wolf, but the Indian was bleeding, and she had to stop it before he bled to death. Maybe if she saved his life, he would take her home. She almost laughed at herself. If she had any brains, she would just get on that horse and ride home. "No, I cannot. What a fool I am to stay, especially after how my father died."

Katrina got up to leave, but the whine of the wolf, as if he was begging for his master's life, stopped her. "Okay, boy, I will stay, but if you so much as lick your chops at me, I am out of here."

At times, Katrina wasn't sure if he was alive or not. It seemed that all she did was make trip after trip down to the creek. It took her forever to get the fire moved over by him. Since he was so big, she couldn't take him to the fire.

As dawn approached, Katrina found herself exhausted. Unbelievably, the wolf allowed her to clean his wounds as well. She just wanted to sit for a minute. A minute was all she needed, and then she would collect some herbs to make a broth for him. He would need some nourishment of some sort.

When Katrina awoke, it was night again. She felt disorientated at first, then she saw the Indian lying with his wolf next to him, and it all came back to her.

As she went to get up, her skin felt on fire from being exposed to the sun all day. She couldn't believe she had slept without being disturbed. She immediately went to the Indian to see if he was still alive. His breathing was shallow; she put a hand to his forehead and couldn't believe how hot he was.

Again, she went to the creek and got some cold water. He would probably die from dehydration from her negligence rather than the wounds.

Trying to put drops of water in his mouth was like working with a defiant child. He didn't want to cooperate at all.

Katrina was surprised at how quickly she fell back to sleep a few hours later.

The following morning, his fever seemed worse. "I do not know what to do with you." Katrina felt helpless. She went to the creek again and soaked the blanket he had on his horse. She draped the blanket on him, hoping the wetness would help. There was shade but not where he was, and she just couldn't budge him, so she kept positioning his horse to block the sun.

Katrina collected some herbs for a soup to dribble into his mouth instead of the water. She felt it might help. This worrying was exhausting.

A good scrubbing in the creek was what she needed. The water felt good on her sunburned skin. She missed her hat to shield her face. She was probably going to develop freckles all over her face, and then Chad would really think of her as a child.

She didn't have much of a choice but to put the dress back on since she tore her shirt up. What difference did it make anyway? She got the bloodstain out, and it didn't take long to dry because there was a warm breeze all day. She had no way to tie her hair back. There wasn't any shirt left to tie it with, so she finger combed it as best as she could and let it hang.

She felt 100 percent better when she walked back into camp. "Okay, Mr. Indian, you are going to get better today. After all, I need to get home. My poor mother must be beside herself with worry."

As she was speaking, she saw his eyes flutter. He looked up at the sky. Katrina knew he wasn't seeing anything, but what she saw startled her. His eyes were a shade of gray she had never seen before—almost silver blue. Then his eyes closed, and he was out again. "Well, that's a start," she praised with a little relief.

Late that morning, Katrina looked up totally surprised by the wolf. He had a rabbit in his jowls and dropped it on her lap. "Good boy," she praised the wolf and slowly put her hand to his ear and rubbed. She was delighted when the wolf pushed his head into her hand for the touch. "Good boy," she said again.

Up in a flash, she put together a rabbit soup. The nourishment was going to be so important when he awoke. He was going to be as weak as a newborn kitten. That would also delay her getting home.

That afternoon, Katrina sat with his head in her lap, dripping broth into his mouth. He seemed to be more responsive, or maybe she was just getting the hang of nursing him.

Once she felt he had a sufficient amount of broth, she wrung out the cloth again and applied it to his forehead. He didn't seem to be nearly as hot anymore, and she was beginning to wonder if he would ever wake up.

"Your touch is tender," he said. When he spoke, she thought she was losing her mind. She couldn't have understood him, could she?

"Wha-what . . . what did you say?" Katrina had frozen at his words. She had understood him, and when she saw the smile on his face, she knew for sure she wasn't hallucinating. But he didn't answer her. He was out again.

"Of all the nerve." She grinned. He had understood her the whole time and had been playing with her. Well, two could play at this game. If nothing else, she was a master at getting even with the men in her life.

Late that afternoon, he started to stir again. Katrina kneeled by him. "Don't move too much. Let the wounds continue to heal. How are you feeling?"

He almost answered; she could see him catch himself. He didn't remember talking to her before, so the game was on. He lay back down and relaxed. Watching her work at the fire got him to thinking about how she wasn't a helpless white woman. She seemed to know the outdoors pretty well. All he could think about was that hair of hers.

Katrina approached him with some more broth. "Here, drink this. It will help you regain your strength." She spoon-fed it into his mouth. "Slowly, you have not had much in your system for four days. Your stomach might want to rebel if you do not go slowly."

With the mention of four days, his eyebrows raised, reminding her again that he understood everything she was saying, and she realized he wasn't that hard to read when his guard was down. What a fool she had been.

After they both ate, Katrina sat with her back to him by the fire. The sun was just setting, and it was a beautiful sight. She was bone-tired after the struggle of keeping him alive. She just wanted to sleep.

Silver Ghost could see how she slumped. He had to admire her for sticking around. No other women would have done that. She could have just left him to die. His respect for her grew another notch.

When it looked as if she was falling asleep in her sitting position, he reached over and tugged on her so she would relax against him instead of the rock.

Immediately, Katrina jumped at his touch. "What are you doing now?" She was so weary she didn't want to play his game anymore. "Look, it seems to me you're strong enough to take care of yourself but not be able to chase after me, so I need to be going now." Before she could think better of it, she mounted his horse. "I am sorry, but I need your horse to get home. I figure he is payment for me saving your life."

Silver Ghost lay back down. His strength was drained. He watched her leaving. He couldn't help but smile at her spunk, and he was about to see it full force.

Katrina spurred his horse, feeling that it was almost too easy. She almost made it to the creek when she heard a shrill whistle, none like she had ever heard before. She didn't even have time to blink an eye when the horse turned to answer the call. It was all she could do to stay on his back.

"Whoa, whoa, damn it, horse. I said stop." But he didn't stop. That creature just kept on going until it stopped right in front of him.

Katrina was fuming with anger. "You think you are pretty clever, do you? Well, I don't need your horse to get where I want to go. I have got two perfectly good legs, and I will still be home before you could travel." With that said, she turned and stomped off. At the last minute, she added, "And if I were you, I would not even try to come after me. With all my brothers and ranch hands, you would not get close."

He couldn't let her leave in the dark. "Wait," came his defeated request.

"Wait, wait." She turned on her heel and pierced him with her eyes. "What do you mean wait?"

"Just what I said. Do not go." He had a sheepish grin on his face. "I am not strong enough to take care of myself," he defended.

She started to leave again, so he suggested, "I will make you a deal. Stay with me for a couple more days, then I will take you home, or at least close to it. I do not want you traveling all that way by yourself. It is the least I can do for all you have done for me."

He knew he owed her that much, but all of a sudden, he wasn't sure he wanted her to go. He could see her thinking about his offer. The wheels were spinning in her pretty little head.

"If you think I am going to trust you after the way you played me for a fool, think again. On the other hand, I am not looking forward to that long trip back on foot and without my gun. I am not too good with a knife. I need my gun."

"I will give you my word."

"For all that is worth," she replied crankily. Damn, she was tired. "Your word is about as good as a pile of manure in a cow pasture."

He had the nerve to laugh at her, so she continued her rampage. "How dare you laugh at me, and how is it you know my language? Mr . . . Mr . . . What is your name anyway?" she asked, out of breath.

"You change the subject quick enough. I thought we were talking about trust." He smiled at her warmly.

"Talk about changing the subject. You're avoiding my questions."

"Okay, okay, I am a good student, and when the white tracker came to our camp, I learned as much as I could from him. My people call me Silver Ghost. What do your people call you?"

"Katrina," she answered quickly then asked, "did you get your name from the color of your eyes?"

"In a way, that had something to do with it. A brave has to earn his name, and my eyes just added to the name I earned." He liked talking to her; she was easy on the eyes and easy to talk with.

"How did you earn your name?"

"When hunting with my grandfather, I could be as quiet as a ghost, so he named me."

She had to laugh at that one. "You were not so quiet the day you tackled me. I heard you break two twigs."

"Ya, well, you win some and you lose some." He sat and thought for a second. "Your name is beautiful, Katrina, but if you were to live with me, I would call you Moonglow."

"Moonglow," Katrina tried the name on for size. "I like that, but why would you give me such a name?"

"When the moon is full, your hair glows, as it is doing now. I have never seen such beautiful hair." Katrina smiled at that. "Your smile is also beautiful."

Katrina got up feeling very uncomfortable. "Why did you not talk to me before?"

"I am not sure. I guess partly because you were dressed as a boy. I was curious about you and wanted to see your true colors. For someone so little, you are so brave."

She blushed to this. "So did you see my true colors?"

"Yes, along with the other spirit in you." He smiled at her warmly.

Katrina felt funny talking to him like this. She had been around men all her life but never had she had a conversation like this with anyone. She had tried to get Chad to talk with her, but he always made her feel like she was being a pest. She wasn't sure what to make of a conversation like this. If she didn't know better, she would say he was flirting with her.

"Come sit by me again," he requested while patting the ground next to him.

"No, I do not think so." Her voice quivered.

"I promise I will not kiss you again, unless you want me to," he teased. "Come on. I need to lean against you. This rock is getting really hard."

"Unless I want you to. Well, there is no chance in that." And just to prove it to him, she went and sat by him.

He laid his head on her lap. Katrina was a little uneasy with this. When he had been unconscious, it was safe. Right now, she didn't feel so safe, then she chuckled to herself when she looked down to find him already fast asleep.

CHAPTER THREE

Chad and his men continued to search for a total of five days. He was ready to pull his hair out. The men were saying as little as possible for fear he would bite their heads off.

Late in the afternoon, they came to another creek. Chad was worried it would take them another day going up and down this creek to find where the tracks started up on the other side.

They all dismounted and started looking. It had become a known routine by now what was expected and what it would take to find the tracks on the other side.

Five minutes later, Paul, one of the hands, ran up to Chad. Out of breath, he explained, "There's a woman and an Indian camped over yonder, just east of here. Do you want to question them?"

"What do we have to lose? Did they see you?" Chad questioned.

"No, I just looked through some shrubs and saw them eating their supper."

The men headed toward the direction in which Paul led them. As they approached, they heard a woman's laughter. The laughter sounded like Katrina's, but when they looked through the shrubs, they saw a woman and an Indian.

"That ain't her," Joe spoke up. "She does not have hair that long."

"Hair, forget the hair. She does not have a body like that," Paul added.

Bo pushed his way through the men to look through the shrubs, saying, "Let me see. She does have long hair. She just keeps it hidden in her hat."

Bo got on his stomach and looked. "The hell it ain't. That is Katrina. Damned if it ain't, Chad."

All the men were lying in their stomachs, gawking. Chad pushed his way into the shrubs. He couldn't believe his eyes. That was Katrina? What happened to the kid in the boy's clothes?

Paul gave a low whistle. "Man, she's been keeping a lot more than that hair of hers under wraps. Look at that body. It might be small, but it sure is . . ." He didn't get to finish his thoughts because of the elbow he got in his ribs from Bo.

Chad was thankful for Bo's handling it because Paul would have gotten worse if he was next to him.

Bo started to rise, but Chad grabbed his arm. "Let's just observe for a while. Let's make sure she is not in any danger before we go charging in."

As they watched, it seemed like Katrina was there of her own free will. No one seemed to be holding her hostage. She appeared to have free rein. She wasn't bound in any way.

Chad couldn't believe his eyes as he watched her. She was definitely a woman now. Who would have thought she could conceal all that hair? He couldn't remember ever seeing hair like that. But the body had him dumbfounded. How could she hide all that? How horrible is it that she felt she had to. She must have bound herself all the time. Why? Why would she feel the need? She was nineteen now. Wasn't she wanting to get married? She needed to start acting like a woman, thinking about it at least.

Chad noticed that the Indian had gone to sleep. "It is time to make our move." Bo started to get up again. Chad stopped him. "Let me go in and get her quietly. I want him to stay asleep as long as possible."

They all nodded in agreement.

Katrina's back was to Chad as he approached. He firmly cupped his hand over her mouth. She froze, and he whispered, "Shhh, it is Chad." He could feel her relax, so he loosened his hold on her.

As she turned in his arms, she saw Silver Ghost come up on Chad from behind with his knife.

"No!" she screamed. It was too late; all hell broke lose. Silver Ghost had his knife at Chad's throat, but before he knew what hit him, Bo, Paul, Bart, and Jay were tackling Silver Ghost to the ground. Then the wolf was there bounding into camp, snarling, ready to attack.

Katrina shrieked, "Stop it. Stop it at once, all of you. Someone is going to get hurt. I said stop it." No one was listening. She was at her wit's end, so she did the first thing that came to mind. She grabbed someone's gun.

She didn't know whose, just the first one she saw, and shot a couple of times into the air.

That brought a stop to the jumbled bodies. They all just stared up at her. She looked from one to the other with murder in her eyes.

She pointed the gun at each one of them as she talked to them like they were naughty little boys. Bart was first because he was kind of on top. "Get up. Now you." She was pointing at Jay. "Okay, the rest of you, stand up. I cannot believe you. I yelled at you to stop. Now look at you, Silver Ghost. Your arm is bleeding again." The wolf growled deep, ready to attack again.

Everyone looked at the man she called Silver Ghost then back to her. They could really care less about him, but the wolf was still a threat. "Calm your animal, or I will shoot him," Chad informed the Indian in a stern voice.

Silver Ghost made a hand signal to the wolf, who lay down next to him.

Bo growled, "Did he take you against your will, Katrina?"

"Well, yes, at first." She looked confused. "What a stupid question."

"What do you mean at first? Have you decided to stay with him?" The anger in Bo's voice was very evident. Katrina could only imagine what he was thinking. Their father's death was by an Indian's arrow.

Chad didn't like the way this conversation was going. "Never mind what you have decided. You are going home with us."

Katrina wasn't taking orders from anyone anymore. "First, I am going to get him back on the road to recovery, then we will talk about going home." *Home* sounded so good to her right now. Sleeping in her own bed sounded so good right now.

Silver Ghost didn't like this man who had his hand around Moonglow's waist. "Who is this man?" he demanded.

"He is a friend." Katrina realized Chad was next to her with his hand on her waist. She backed away feeling a little self-conscious.

"What kind of friend?" Silver Ghost gritted his teeth.

"An old friend of the family," she answered coolly.

Chad looked at her with surprise on his face. "I do not consider myself that old, Katrina." He winked at her.

"Oh, stop this, both of you. Silver Ghost, you go sit down. I will bandage you up again." She glared at all of them as she said *again*.

Chad grabbed her arm. "Let one of the men do it. I want a word with you."

"If you want to walk again, Chad Miles, you had better let go of my arm this instant."

Silver Ghost snickered at this. She was definitely a little hellcat.

Chad's and Katrina's eyes locked. Although she looked like a whole different person, she was still the same old bossy Katrina. He had to give her credit. She knew her own mind.

As Katrina was bandaging Silver Ghost again, he was trying to talk to her, but there were too many ears and eyes on them. She worked quickly and efficiently while the others watched like hawks. She didn't know what they thought Silver Ghost was going to do with all of them standing guard.

Chad watched with a tightening in his gut he couldn't quite place. He was anxious for her to be done. Watching her tenderly bandage the Indian was unnerving to say the least.

Irritably, he asked, "Can we have that talk now?"

"Sure." She shrugged. "Let's take a walk."

Silver Ghost watched as they walked off. He was seeing red.

The walk was quiet at first. Neither said anything, lost in their own thoughts. Chad wasn't sure how to broach the question he needed to ask, but if he didn't get a satisfying answer, he would be hanging an Indian tonight, with or without Katrina's blessings.

When Chad stopped and faced her, he had an overwhelming need to just hold her, so he pulled her into his arms before she could protest.

Rather than protest, she began to shake. The shaking became so violent as if she was going into shock. "What is this?" he asked as he pulled her closer.

Katrina wasn't sure why she was shaking; she just knew she couldn't stop. Being in Chad's arms felt good.

Chad held her tight. "You are safe now. He will not hurt you anymore." He lifted her chin to look into her eyes. "Trina." It was the pet name that only he called her, and it had been a long time since he had used it.

His voice cracked with emotion, "I have to ask." He fidgeted. He just had to blurt it out. "Did he?" God, this was hard. Her eyes were wide. "Did he rape you?"

He felt her stiffen in his arms; sure, she was going to say yes.

"No, Chad, he did not." She could see the disbelief on his face. "He was attacked by a mountain lion the first night and was unconscious up until last night." She wasn't about to offer that the possibility was definitely there.

Then he smiled. "Good. I am glad. I really did not want to have to kill him along with those brothers of yours."

She chuckled. "Well, as far as my brothers go, you will have to stand in line behind me, and by the time I am finished with them, there will not be much left of their hides for you to take off."

He pulled her close again. "That is my Trina."

"I like the sound of that."

"What is that?" She had stopped shaking. That was a good thing. Holding her felt like a good thing. He couldn't explain it.

"You calling me Trina. It has been a couple of years."

"It fit you when you were younger, and somehow it fits you dressed up as a woman. By the way . . ." He pushed her away and held her at arm's length to get a good look at her. "Where in the world have you been hiding all this?" He held out her hair, as he looked at her body up and down.

Katrina blushed wildly. "Ain't this pretty disgusting?" She looked down at herself. This thing fit even tighter since she had washed it in the stream to get the bloodstains out.

"It is pretty something all right, but *disgusting* is not the word I would use to describe it." He winked at her as the word *sexy* came to mind.

Again, she turned three shades of red. They were looking into each other's eyes. She wanted him to kiss her so much and was certain he was going to when they heard a gunshot.

"No!" Katrina screamed as they both took off running for the campsite. There was another shot, then another. Katrina's blood was turning cold. Why was it taking so long to get back to camp? It didn't seem like they had walked that far from camp, and it was taking forever to get back.

Finally arriving, they saw the men doing some target practice. Everyone was safe. Again, Katrina started to shake.

Chad could see her shaking and pulled her close again. He was afraid she was worried about the Indian, and that was disturbing to him.

Silver Ghost hadn't relaxed since she had walked out of the camp, into the dark, with the man they were calling Chad, but now that she was back and being held by that man, he wanted to hit something or someone.

Silver Ghost needed to get her attention without actually calling out her name, so he moaned, as if in pain, and she was by his side in an instant.

"Are you okay?" She knelt beside him. She wrung out the cloth and dabbed it on his forehead. "Just relax. I am here." She sat down, and he laid his head on her lap.

She felt very uncomfortable with everyone watching. Her eyes locked with Chad's, and she could tell he didn't like it one bit. It was evident when he marched over to his horse and took off the saddle blanket. Then he marched over and tossed it on the ground next to them.

"Here, use this." He ground out then headed for the creek. He was just itching to hit that guy. If Katrina weren't so determined to get him well and on his way, he would hurt him and hurt him bad. He knew what was on the guy's mind; he could read it in his eyes. Over Chad's dead body would that Indian have Katrina.

When Silver Ghost fell asleep, Katrina walked down to the creek. She didn't need a light anymore. She had walked this path a hundred times in the last five days.

She spotted Chad sitting on a boulder, looking out over the water. She had been so quiet she startled him when she spoke.

"Everything okay?" Her voice was soft and warm, but it sent a chill up his spine. She was scaring the hell out of him right now. Something was totally different tonight with her. She wasn't the little girl he was used to being around, and it felt strange thinking of her as a woman, but he couldn't deny the body that was standing before him.

"Can I sit down, or do you have claim to that rock?"

Chad moved over and patted the rock next to him. "Have a seat."

She sat then waited for him to say something. She was just to the point where she felt she would have to break the silence when he spoke.

"I am taking you home first thing in the morning."

She started to protest, and he put his fingers on her lips.

"Please do not argue. Your ma has got to be going out of her mind by now. I left her in tears, Trina. She needs to see you are okay with her own eyes."

She knew he was right, but what would happen to Silver Ghost?

"Do you have any idea what your hair does in the moonlight?"

"Ya, it glows," she supplied glumly.

"How did you know that?" It was exactly the word he was trying to think of.

"Silver Ghost, that is his name by the way, said that would be a name that would fit me."

He hadn't been able to concentrate since she sat down next to him. He needed to get her away from here, away from that Indian.

"Look, Trina, I think that guy has had an opportunity to sweet-talk you, and I know for a fact it is the first time you have had anyone sweet-talk you. Partly because you have never dressed as a woman or given anyone else a chance. Now that I know what you have been hiding all this time, it is going to be very hard for me to look at you as a child again. Not when I know there is a woman's body under your cowboy hat, and a beautiful one at that. I cannot believe you were able to conceal all this perfection."

Katrina didn't know what to say. These were words she had always hoped to hear from Chad. If she would have known he wanted a woman, she might have been more prone to dress in a dress once in a while, but she had always heard him swear off women.

Chad couldn't explain anything tonight, but he knew he had a need to kiss her—if for no other reason than to show her what a real kiss could be like. He had a feeling this Silver Ghost had kissed her, and she was in awe of her first kiss on the lips. He had to show her there were other feelings too.

Before he could second think himself, he pulled her into his lap and kissed her with all the emotion he could muster. It didn't take much, because once their lips touched and she responded to him, he deepened the kiss and was lost. He couldn't tell how long they kissed because it seemed like hours—hours of ecstasy.

Their foreheads touched. "Trina?"

"Hmm?"

"I'm not sorry I just kissed you." And he really wasn't.

"*Wow*! I'm not either, Chad." The smile that was spreading across her face was contagious.

"I should get you back before I ruin your reputation."

With that, she laughed. "What reputation?"

"The one you are going to have when I get you home."

"What do you mean?"

"Think about it. You have been out for five days with an Indian. No one is going to believe you were spared your innocence."

"But I was." Her body stiffened.

"Let's just deal with one issue at a time, one day at a time." All of a sudden, he felt so tired. It seemed the last week of work and worry had finally caught up with him.

"Let's get back to the others and get a good night's shut-eye. We have a long ride ahead of us tomorrow." He couldn't let things get out of hand with her. He was getting in too deep over his head. Mrs. Holt would never forgive him for rescuing her from her abductor and then taking advantage of her himself.

The following morning was just as Chad said it would be. Her brother and the three hands were staying behind to see to it that Silver Ghost was able to head to his camp, and she and Chad were heading home to the ranch.

Chad was already on his horse, and Katrina was mounting when she heard "Moonglow." It was Silver Ghost.

Chad didn't like the pet name the Indian had given her. Although it suited her, he didn't like anything intimate between those two.

"I will be right back," she told Chad.

As she knelt by Silver Ghost, he reached up and pulled her down to whisper in her ear. "If your friends had not shown up, I would have had you."

She never had a chance to comment on his words because he pulled her to him and was kissing her with so much force she almost felt dizzy.

Chad was in a rage and off his horse so fast he thought he would fall on his face. He grabbed Katrina from behind and pulled her out of the Indian's arms. His veins were popping out of his neck as he spoke. "If you ever lay a hand on her again, I will personally pull your arms out of your body."

Chad was holding Katrina so hard she thought he was going to demonstrate what he said he would do right then and there. She twisted out of his grasp. "You are hurting me," she hissed.

Chad's eyes never left Silver Ghost. "Get on your horse, Katrina."

"But . . ."

His tone left no room for argument, "Now!" He then faced Silver Ghost. "She is off limits to you. Do I make myself clear?" He didn't wait for an answer; he just turned around and headed for the horses.

When he got there, Katrina hadn't gotten all the way on her horse, so he finished putting her in the saddle with a thud.

She started to protest.

"Do not say a word," he warned.

They rode out, and she kept her silence.

The ride was quiet. They had been riding for thirty minutes, and he felt a little more relaxed. The sight of her being mauled by that Indian wouldn't leave his mind, but the irritation was melting away.

Every now and then, he would look over at her, and the expressions he was seeing on her face were as different as night and day. At one moment, she had anger, then worry, sometimes even a smile, but that wouldn't last long she would go right back to anger. He could tell she was mostly angry and knew that when she let loose, there was going to be hell to pay.

Her poor horse, Trader, didn't know if she wanted him to run, walk, trot, or what. It seemed whatever she was thinking about, the horse was commanded to go with her mood; her pace kept varying. Right now, he could tell she was angry again because she was at a run.

At the ranch, when something was eating at her, she would go out and kick a few bales of hay. He needed a way to unleash that anger before she exploded.

He rode up next to her, and she looked over at him. "What are you thinking, Chad?"

"About how I'm going to help you release some of that tension." He had a smirk on his face.

"I am not tense." Her veins were sticking out on her neck as she lied. "Chad" was all she got out before he pulled her off her horse, and they both hit the ground. She couldn't believe she was eating dirt again.

"What are you doing?" she demanded.

Chad stood and pulled her to her feet. "I want you to hit me."

"What?" She was stunned.

"Come on, hit me." He was smiling. Damn, she looked good in that dress.

"I most certainly will not, and wipe that expression off your face, or I will hit you." She was so annoyed with him.

"What expression? This one? Or this one?" He was making all kinds of faces at her as he was dancing around with his dukes up. "Come on, hit me."

"Chad, stop it!" She was starting to laugh.

He gave her a little shove. "Come on, Trina, show me what ya got."

"Okay, you asked for it." She swung wide and missed him just as he ducked.

"Oh, you can do better than that. I know you can?"

He was teasing her, and he knew she didn't like to be teased. The anger was returning again. He could see it in her face. As she swung this time, she connected with his gut.

Chad doubled over out of breath. "Oh, that was a good one."

Katrina was shocked that he had pushed her far enough to really want to hit him and hit him hard. "Chad, are you all right? I really did not mean to hurt you, but you would not shut up and you kept asking for it." She was standing next to him, holding his arm.

Chad looked at her sideways then smiled as he sprang up laughing. "Just kidding. Fooled you. You hardly touched me." He was jumping all over the place; she could hardly keep up with him. She had never seen this playful side of him. He was always all business at home.

"Is that right? Well, you better be prepared because I am not holding back this time." Then she bent over and charged him like a bull and planted her head right in his stomach. They both flew to the ground in a thud with Katrina landing on top.

The shocked look on her face was more than Chad could stand. He burst out laughing. She followed suit, laughing uncontrollably, and miraculously, she felt better.

Chad rolled her off him to lie next to him, then he rolled on his side and propped himself up on his elbow. Katrina remained on her back with her eyes closed and a big smile on her face.

"Do you feel better, Trina?" he asked. His breath was so close to her ear, and his voice was a whisper that gave her chills.

She turned her head to look at him, and their mouths almost touched. She realized she wanted him to kiss her again.

"Trina, when that Indian kissed you, he was taking advantage of your inexperience. Men can be very convincing with a kiss. So can a woman who knows what she is doing." He felt flustered trying to explain things to her. She was definitely inexperienced in these things. He knew she had never been kissed before and was reading too much into the kiss. Damn. Out of frustration, he took her in his arms and kissed her with all the lust he could muster.

At first, Katrina didn't know what to think when his tongue entered her mouth, but the more he kissed her, the more she liked it, and it was totally different than when Silver Ghost kissed her. Chad seemed to give and take, whereas Silver Ghost only took.

Katrina was the first to pull away. "What does this mean, Chad?"

"What? The kissing?" He tried really hard to sound nonchalant. Katrina nodded. "Well, I wanted to show you that a kiss could be what you want it to be. That Indian was taking advantage of you, and I do not want you falling for him over some damn kiss. This kiss meant nothing, yet it felt good and was convincing enough to seem like it meant something, but it did not. You are like a kid sister to me, nothing more."

She couldn't believe her ears. "You mean to tell me you felt nothing in that kiss?" She was angry all over again. She was still in his arms and wanted to escape. She shoved out of his grasp and yelled, "Let go of me, Chad. Now!"

As he stood, he reached to help her up, but she slapped his hand away. "I can get up myself." He could tell she was spitten mad.

He could tell he had hurt her, but there was no other way, and no matter what, he would never admit he was on fire for her. "Katrina" was all he got out before she sucker punched him in the nose.

"Take that you, you, ewe . . ." She couldn't finish. She just got on Trader and took off, yelling over her shoulder, "I hate you, Chad Miles. You let me make a fool of myself. It would serve you right if I went back to Silver Ghost."

She kicked Trader harder. She wanted to be as far away from Chad as she could get. She would never let him see that he had brought tears to her eyes. That made her angry. She hardly ever cried. He would be sorry for the day he ever kissed her.

He knew he had hurt her, but it was for the best. If she had any idea of how much she curled his toes when she kissed him back like that. She could call him the liar that he was, but he had no intentions on letting her know any of that.

A while later, Chad had caught up with her. He knew she wouldn't run her horse into the ground.

They rode quietly for quite some time, then Katrina blurted out, "I need to hit something again."

"Well, I am not volunteering this time. You will have to wait until we get home."

"Do not worry. If the outcome were to be the same, I would prefer someone with feelings." Then she took off again, wanting to get home as soon as possible.

Chad just smiled to himself. It was better for her to hate him. He quietly mumbled, "Oh, I have feelings all right, my little Trina. I have feelings."

CHAPTER FOUR

It was getting dark. They had ridden through lunch, and they were both exhausted. "Trina, let's rest at the watering hole. The horses need a break.

As much as she hated to admit it, he was right.

By the time they reached the watering hole, it was completely dark. "Let's make camp here for the night, Trina."

"Do not call me that."

He continued, "The horses are tired, and so is my back." He expected an argument, some kind of disapproval from her, but she just got off her horse without a word.

She knew they were really close to home, but she didn't think she could go any further tonight anyway.

Chad went about setting up a camp. He built a fire, laid out the bedroll, took the saddles off their horses, and put some potatoes on the grill.

He stopped and looked around but didn't see Katrina anywhere. "Trina," he hollered out, but she didn't answer. "Trina!" he called and headed out into the dark then stopped dead in his tracks.

"Do you mind if I have a little privacy? Can't a girl go to the bathroom?"

If she could have seen his face, she would have seen him turn three shades of red, and he couldn't remember the last time he had been embarrassed. As he backed up, he said, "Sorry, Trina. You should have answered me when I called. I was worried." He was stumbling all over himself trying to talk.

"Would you mind turning around and leaving me alone?" she shouted at him.

He did just that too. He couldn't exit fast enough. What a fool he felt like, but it was her own fault for not answering.

They ate in silence. Chad didn't know what to say to her. He didn't want to start another argument, and he could tell by her body language that she was still angry with him.

Katrina couldn't believe she had melted in his arms the way she had. His kisses felt so good to her. How could he have not felt anything? Who was he to think he could play with her this way? He could have just explained to her that kisses could be faked with emotion. She would hate him forever, although it seemed like she had loved him forever already.

They both cleaned up the dinner mess, then Chad went to fill his canteen. When he returned, Katrina had already fallen asleep.

Chad quietly walked to the rock and sat down. From where he sat, the fire cast a glow on her that seemed to bring out an angelic picture.

He should cover her up, but he was enjoying the picture too much. Like a soft cloud, her hair fell all around her. The Indian dress hugged her body in all the right places. He couldn't believe this was the same little girl that had been stirring up trouble last week. She had grown into a woman overnight, and all those curves had been hidden so well. Damn, his body was reacting to this woman lying in front of him, and a woman she definitely was. No, she was a little sister, *remember?* This was nuts.

Chad abruptly got up and threw a blanket on her. He was not going to pursue these feelings that were stirring inside him, but it was the first time he could ever remember wishing he wasn't so close to the Holt family.

She was no doubt a beauty and would make some man very happy. She really had it all: spunky, pretty, good, sexy, beautiful, ornery, gorgeous, prideful, wonderful, cocky, and again, *very* sexy. There, his mind went again. He knew he couldn't let these feelings be known. She deserved better than him, better than just some ranch hand. She deserved someone who could give her all the things she could ever dream of. Hell, he didn't have a pot to piss in. There was nothing he could offer her.

She would need a husband that could give her more than he would ever be able to provide. *Husband?* Now where did that come from? He was never getting married again. He swore off women long ago. To get wrapped up in one female was just asking for trouble.

He needed to go to sleep. His mind was getting warped. That was it. He was just overtired. Things would look differently in the morning. She would be that little sister again.

Chad looked at Katrina's sleeping form. He felt the chill in the air. The night was cooler than he had expected, and there was only one blanket. He knew he was borrowing trouble, but they would need each other's body heat to stay warm, so he lay down next to her.

Sleep didn't come easy for Chad, especially when she cuddled up into the crook of his arm. He lay really still so as to not wake her, and damned if she didn't seem to fit just right in the crook of his arm. It was as if she were made for him. Then she draped her leg over his and snuggled even closer. She was going to be his undoing. He needed to put some space between them.

Chad rolled so his back was to her, but that didn't detour her. She just cuddled him like a spoon. He was okay; he could get through this. One night being next to her wouldn't change his mind about anything. He just needed to get some sleep. After all, she was like a little sister.

Chad woke with a start. "Trina?" he whispered. She wasn't next to him, and immediately, he felt empty. "Don't even think about it," he berated himself. "Damn, that girl. Where was she now?"

The gunshot brought him to his knees; he scrambled behind a boulder and felt a fear in his gut as he reached for his gun in his holster, just to find it missing. "Trina, where are you?" he hollered. Did he sleep so hard someone came into camp and kidnapped her right out from under his nose, taking his gun with them? "Trina!" he hollered louder this time.

"What?" she asked sweetly as she walked into camp, carrying a dead rabbit by the ears. Cocky pride was all over her face.

"What do you think you're doing scaring the hell out of me?"

"Getting us some breakfast. Ain't he a dandy?" She held up her kill and just beamed.

She was so amazing. Chad couldn't do anything but just slump against the boulder, shaking. He didn't know if it was from laughing or from the rush of adrenaline, out of fear for her safety that had pumped through his veins seconds ago.

Chad sat and watched as she prepared their breakfast.

Katrina could feel him watching her. She felt so alive this morning when she had woken up. She was on her right side, and behind her was Chad cuddling her. He was snoring gently in her ear, one arm holding her close and one leg draped over her. She felt safe and protected. It felt good.

When she tried to get up, he had mumbled, "Uh-uh, you feel good." And he pulled her even closer.

She was content to just lie there with him holding her, as if they were a married couple, until she couldn't deny Mother Nature another minute.

When she did unravel herself from his embrace, she looked at him sleeping, and he had a smile on his face. "This I could get used to," she promised herself.

Now she was fixing him breakfast, and she repeated those words, "This I could get used to." She really didn't mean to voice it out loud, but she must have.

He asked, "What was that?"

Embarrassed, Katrina busied herself even more. "Oh, I was talking to the rabbit," she lied.

He was starting to make her nervous watching her. She felt clumsy all of a sudden and sloshed the coffee on her hand. "Ow!" she cried.

Chad was by her side in a heartbeat. "Are you okay?" He took her hand in his. It wasn't bad. He saw that she had some water in a bowl, so he stuck her hand in it. The water was plenty cold to take the sting away. Chad looked up to see her watching him. Their eyes met, and his heart skipped a beat.

Chad cleared his throat. "Is that better?" he asked, unable to look away.

Katrina couldn't feel the pain in her hand, but she could sure feel the pull of her heart. She found herself leaning toward him, wanting him to kiss her more than anything. This was all so new to her. She never thought she'd see the day when she and Chad could be intimate, and sleeping next to him all night felt like more than being a sister. This had been something she had wanted for so long, but he had never noticed her before now.

Katrina closed her eyes for the kiss she knew he was going to give her, but that was when Chad came to his senses. He stood up abruptly.

Totally tongue-tied, he mumbled something about getting her to safety.

The two of them started out for home after breakfast. Katrina wasn't going to let Chad's semi rejection destroy her high spirits.

Chad noticed how happy she seemed to be. "Your ma will be glad you are home safely, Trina."

She just smiled at him.

"I bet you will be glad to see her again. I bet you thought you would never see her again."

Again she just smiled at him.

They continued to ride in silence for a while, then Chad asked, "Have you decided how you are going to pay back those brothers of yours over this practical joke?"

He was looking for conversation, but she wasn't going to oblige. Her answers were short and sweet. "Not yet." She just smiled again.

"Well, it ought to be good after all you have been through."

Again, she just smiled. She was starting to rattle his nerves. What was with her? It wasn't like her to be so vague.

"You want a piece of jerky?" Chad offered.

"No, thank you," she said, smiling.

He couldn't read her mood. "Trina, have I done something to make you mad at me again?"

"Not at all, Chad," she responded nonchalantly.

"Can we ride faster, Chad? I am anxious to get home."

Chad realized he was taking his time, wanting to prolong their time being alone. He didn't want to even rationalize that one. "I will race you," he said.

Before he could even finish his sentence, she was at a fast run. "Hey, you cheat!" he yelled after her.

He wasn't worried about catching her. She was a good rider, but he was better.

Chad watched her from behind. Her hair flying out behind her was a sight to be seen. He was still amazed that all this had been hidden for so long. How did someone stuff that much hair into a hat? How did she conceal all those curves? How could he have been so blind? That ranch hand he had to let go of a while back had a lot more sense than he did. That kid had seen what Katrina had been hiding all along. How was it that Chad had missed the change?

He was drawn back to the present when he heard Katrina hoot with laughter.

She had run right through a herd of cattle and stirred them all up. She was a she-cat at heart. She was radiant, and she was starting to stir him up again.

Katrina could hear Chad catching up to her. She kicked harder, wanting so bad to beat him home.

Chad rode up beside her and saw the determined look on her face. She was bent over, riding as one with her horse. He couldn't help himself.

He grabbed her off her horse, and they both tumbled to the ground again. Chad landed on top of her.

When Katrina finally got her lungs full of air again, she let him have it. "You idiot, you could have killed me."

"No chance of that." He smiled at her.

"Get off me," she grunted.

"No chance of that either." He smiled down at her. She was looking at his lips, and he couldn't stop himself. He lowered his mouth to hers. The kiss started out rough but turned to heat in a hurry. She was floating in heaven, kissing him back with all the love she had to give. Then she remembered his word *sister*, so she grabbed the back of his head by the hair and pulled his mouth away from hers, struggling to get out from under him.

Chad released her, and when she stood up, she was fuming. "How dare you?" she scolded then slapped him good and hard.

"I guess I deserved that?" He had a smile on his face while he rubbed his cheek where it smarted.

"You bet your life you did. None of my brothers ever kissed me like that. If I am like a little sister to you, why would you kiss me at all?"

Fortunately for Chad, she stomped off, mounted her horse, and left him in the dust. He didn't have to come up with an answer.

Twenty minutes later, they rode up into the compound. Katrina's mother was out the door in a flash. Someone had hollered that riders were coming in, and she didn't waste a second.

Katrina jumped off her horse and ran into her mother's arms.

"Oh, Katrina, you gave me such a fright." Her mom was crying as she held her tight. "Let me look at you. Are you all right? Are you hurt?" As her mom's eyes widened, she asked, "What on earth are you wearing? What have you done with my daughter? Who is this beautiful creature pretending to be my daughter?"

Katrina laughed to lighten the mood. "Oh, Mama, stop it. I am okay. I really was not in danger. It was just an interesting adventure." Katrina looked at Chad as she said this to her ma.

Evelyn held out her arms to Chad. "I need a group hug."

Chad reluctantly walked into the folds of Evelyn's arms. Katrina wrapped one arm around his middle and the other arm around her mama's waist. With Chad in the middle of the two of them, Katrina whispered, "Thank you for coming after me." And she kissed his cheek so softly.

The brush of her lips on his cheek, the whispering in his ear, made him feel sad—sad that more couldn't have come of their *adventure*—but he would not have taken advantage of Katrina. He cared for her too much.

Evelyn started to shake. Katrina could feel it. "Mama, what's wrong?"

"Oh, honey, I thought I was never going to see my baby girl again. You were gone for so long. I was beginning to think the worst. I prayed every minute of the day, but as each day went by, I was beginnin' to give up hope." She looked at Chad while crying openly. "Thank you so much for bringin' my little girl home to me. I do not think I could have endured losing her."

"You are very welcome. Now let's get you inside and get a warm cup of coffee in you. You are chilled." Chad didn't think her shaking had anything to do with the chill in the air. People tended to shake from emotion or fear of the unknown. He knew this woman was strong, but to lose another loved one so soon after her husband's death, let alone her only daughter, it could have been her undoing.

Katrina watched as Chad helped her mom into the house. She knew her mom was shaking from the sheer relief of her safety. Watching Chad take care of her mom only made her care for him more. He was such a good man. She wanted more than anything to show him she could be a good woman. She would start today.

That evening, there was to be a big welcome-home party for Katrina. Evelyn needed something to calm her nerves, and cooking was her best medicine. She cooked all day, preparing a feast for a king. She wanted Chad to know how much she appreciated him for all the kind deeds he did for this family.

Chad had busied himself around the house. He didn't venture off too far, hoping to see Katrina every now and then. At the noon meal, he had asked Evelyn where Katrina was.

She simply replied, "The poor dear took a hot bath then fell instantly asleep. I guess this adventure was more draining on her than she realized."

Chad couldn't help himself. After they finished eating, he peeked into Katrina's bedroom, and just as her mother said, she was sound asleep. He hoped she wasn't coming down with something. Lord, she was pretty.

"Is anything wrong, Chad?" Evelyn startled him from behind.

"No, no, I was just checking on her. I, um,"—Chad cleared his throat—"I will get back to work."

Evelyn touched his arm. "Chad, she has always had feelings for you, you know?" She had a knowing smile on her face.

"Ya, well, she is just a kid." He tried denying his feelings.

"Ya, well, that kid is not such a kid anymore, Chad, in case you did not notice." Evelyn opened the door a little more. "I would say she is now a woman. How about you, Chad?"

Chad cleared his throat again. "I will just get back to work now." But as he left, he had a feeling he wasn't kidding anyone, including himself.

Katrina couldn't believe it, but she had slept all day. When she awoke, it was already dusk. She could smell all kinds of food: fried chicken, brownies, and other foods that made her mouth just water. She was famished. She dressed in a hurry, threw on some jeans and a sweatshirt, and tucked her hair into her hat.

When she entered the kitchen, her mom welcomed her with a big hug. "I bet you are hungry."

"I am starving, and everything smells wonderful. Could I have a little nibble? I do not want to spoil my dinner, but I do not think I can wait another minute."

"Your brothers and the men will be in in about an hour. I will prepare you a snack. You sit and tell me what is up with Chad?"

Katrina almost stumbled into the chair. "What do you mean, mama?"

"Well, I caught him watching you sleep earlier. Let's just say the look he had on his face was not one of revulsion."

Katrina blushed to her toes. "Oh, Mama, he kissed me, and I don't think I can explain what it did to me, but I care for him more now than I ever did."

Evelyn couldn't be more excited about this news. "I think he cares for you too, Katrina. Problem is, he has thought of you for so long as a kid sister. It is going to take some time for him to come around. He is truly fighting his feelings for you, but I think they are there."

"Oh, Mama, I hope so."

"What do you hope is so?"

Both Katrina and her ma jumped at the sound of Chad's voice. "I see you are back to your old self, Trina."

"In what way?" Katrina asked. She didn't like the tone of his voice.

Chad thumped her hat. "You know, you look like your old self."

All of a sudden, Katrina felt sloppy. She did have a dress or two in her closet. Her mother had always made a couple for her as she grew. She just never wore them. But she wasn't going to have him tell her what she should wear or shouldn't. She would wear whatever she felt like.

"Ya, well, I like my clothes. I do not tell you what to wear."

"I was not telling you what to wear. I like you in your old jeans better than that squaw outfit anyway, but you might find if you wear a dress once in a while you might have a few admirers."

For some reason, she didn't believe that he wanted her to have admirers.

Although the boy's stuff helped him to keep his feelings in check, he didn't think he would ever forget the image of her with her hair flowing all over her back and shoulders or the way that outfit had hugged her beautiful curves.

Chad grabbed an apple and went out the back door.

Evelyn cleared her throat. "Um, Katrina?"

Katrina didn't hear her at first. She was feeling insulted by Chad at the moment.

Her ma tried to get her attention again, but it took stepping in front of her and snapping her fingers to do it. "Katrina, you do have some dresses in your closet. You go and change for dinner?"

"I will not. This is what I have always worn, and I do not plan on changing for anyone."

"Okay, suit yourself. Here is your snack." She set a plate in front of Katrina, but all of a sudden, she didn't have an appetite anymore.

"Men—they think they can tell you what to do. Not me, I will wear whatever I feel like," she mumbled to herself since no one else was in the room.

That evening, they all had a good laugh. Katrina told her brothers they better be watching their backs. She intended to get even when they least expected it.

That evening, at the dinner table, Katrina told everyone what had happened to her from the moment her brothers left her. Her audience was tuned into her every word, while Chad sat on the sidelines, listening to her make them all laugh. The next thing he knew, she was telling them of him kissing her and the lesson in which he was trying to teach her. Chad looked up, shocked by her words, and noticed everyone staring at him.

Chad turned to stone. He was embarrassed, but more than that, he was mad. She was making a laughingstock out of him. He didn't have anything to say, so he excused himself. "Thank you, Mrs. Holt. That was a perfect meal." Chad wiped his mouth once more, threw down his napkin, and left.

Katrina instantly felt the pain she had caused him. She knew his ex-wife had humiliated him in front of a bunch of people. That wasn't what she had intended to do. She just wanted everyone to see how naive she was and laugh at her, but they took it all wrong.

The party broke up shortly after that, and Katrina felt she was the cause.

She helped her ma clean up the mess. Her ma didn't say anything to her until they were almost finished.

"Sometimes when someone has hurt us, we want to hurt them back, but the best advice I can give you is to not do something to someone on purpose to make them mad at you. Life is too short to go around bitter."

"Mama, I did not mean to hurt him. I am sorry. I do not know what to do."

"Do not tell me, honey. Tell him." Her mom knew a little of the relationship with Chad and his ex-wife but only because Chad had shared a little with her late husband, who had shared with her.

"I do not know how, Mama."

"Why, you sleep on it. Maybe tomorrow things will seem a little clearer."

"Thanks, Mama. I love you." Katrina hugged her mom so tightly. She didn't want to let go.

"I love you too, honey. Get a good night's sleep."

Sleep didn't come for Katrina that night. She didn't know if it was because she had slept all day or because her mind wouldn't shut up. All she could think of was how she had hurt Chad. She needed to do something to make it up to him. She just didn't know what.

Two days later, her brother Bo and the other men came in. All seemed to be okay. No one was harmed; everyone was home safe and sound.

Chad had kept his distance from Katrina. She hadn't made an effort to seek him out either. She hadn't come up with a way to apologize to him.

Chad just wanted things to go back to the way they were before all this adventure took place. It was a hard lesson to learn, but he was glad he had come to his senses before he had made a jackass out of himself.

He had tried to tell himself that Katrina was different, but what it all boiled down to was it didn't matter what a woman looked like or did. They were all the same—vengeful.

Chad had been in the barn hitching up the buckboard for Mrs. Holt. His guess was she was going into town, but when he had asked her, she just said it wasn't for her. Chad did what he was asked anyway.

Bo walked in. He and Chad had not had a chance to talk since Bo had gotten home. Not that there was much to talk about, but Chad wanted a couple of answers.

"So did the Indian make it back to his people okay?" Chad asked, hoping they had seen the last of him.

"I right do not know, Chad. He ditched us one night while we was sleepin', so we headed on home."

"I see . . ." Chad looked up to see Katrina walk into the barn. What a vision she made.

"Now I have an answer to my question." Chad was talking to Katrina.

"What question might that be?" she asked coolly.

"Why the buckboard instead of your horse?" Chad took her all in. The dress she wore was a light pink with tiny red roses all over it. It fit to perfection except for one thing—the cleavage was a bit too much.

Bo spoke up, "Katrina, my dear sister, you have quite a package to offer there." Bo made it very clear that he was referring to her bust bulging at the seams in the V-neck line of her dress.

"Why, thank you, brother dear. I do believe I have been overly endowed." It was way too much as far as she was concerned, but with Chad's eyes taking her in the way he was, she all of a sudden felt that she had made the right decision in wearing a dress.

Chad noticed how the dress hugged her tiny waist. He still couldn't believe a person could look so different from one day to the next. The thing that caught his attention the most was her hair. Her mother must have spent hours on it. She had pinned it up in curls, with more curls hanging down her back.

"What do you think, Chad?" Katrina asked him.

"Chad?" Bo piped in, "Chad?"

"Hum? What? Oh, uh, you look mighty fine, Trina." Chad got a hold of himself. This was too much for him; he needed a break.

"Why, thank you, Chad. Is the team hitched?" She pretended his compliment meant nothing, while inside, she was jumping for joy.

Bo watched in amazement. His sister had grown into quite a beauty, and she dazed Chad. Bo was going to have fun watching this relationship blossom. They were both very hardheaded people, used to getting their own way. And the conversation at hand was proving him right.

"Who is going with you, Trina?" Chad was asking.

"No one," she answered innocently.

"You are not going alone," Chad stated matter-of-factly.

"Why not? I have always gone alone in the past." Katrina looked at Chad, annoyed.

"Well, that was when . . . that was before . . . you were not . . . Damn it, Trina. You're dressed as a woman now. You need an escort."

Trina had climbed up onto the seat of the buckboard. She turned with her hands on her hips and glared at Chad. "What? You have got to be joking. Chad, I can take care of myself."

To prove her point, she lifted her skirt to show she was carrying a weapon strapped to her leg. "Chad, whether I am in a dress or pants, I can take care of myself," she said. Her voice was getting louder.

Now Chad's voice was getting even louder, "In pants, you were not drawing attention to yourself. Looking like you do, every head in town will turn."

Katrina's face lit up. That was the nicest compliment he had ever given her. She acted like she hadn't caught to its meaning.

"Well, that is what you want, Chad? Is it not what you said—if I were to wear a dress once in a while, I might have an admirer?" She paused for a second then added, "Are you sure you are not one of my admirers, Chad Miles?" With that, she cracked the reins and left in the buckboard, heading to town *alone*. Boy, she felt good.

Bo started laughing when he saw the expression on Chad's face. "Well, I think she got you there, Chad. It's written all over your face. You're smitten with her, and God, who wouldn't be? If she weren't my sister, I think I might be a little smitten myself."

"Ah, shut up, Bo. Who asked you anyway?" Chad responded with a scowl on his face.

Bo decided to follow Katrina on his horse after all that. What Chad said did make sense. Whether she liked it or not, she needed an escort.

CHAPTER FIVE

Katrina was enjoying her ride into town. The weather was just right. She loved the fall because she loved the trees full of all their colors.

She heard the horse coming up on her, and when she looked and saw it was Bo and not Chad, she was a little disappointed.

Bo just winked at her and said, "Just pretend I am not here." And they rode on in their own thoughts.

In town, she got plenty of reaction to how she was dressed. The men were all tongue-tied, and the women looked at her like she had grown another head.

She had gone into the mercantile to look for some more yardages. Her mother had told her to pick out a couple of prints, and the two of them could work on a dress or two together.

In the mercantile, Mrs. Jenkins approached her with praise, "Why, Katrina dear, I would not have recognized you in a million years. Dear, you are simply beautiful. Come sit down. Let me get you a sarsaparilla."

Katrina sat looking around. Again, the other young women were looking at her strangely. "Here is my list of items."

The older woman handed the list to the stock boy. "Her buckboard's right out front, Dale. Go ahead and fill the order."

"Mrs. Jenkins, is there something out of place on me? I know I look different, but some of the looks I am getting seem hateful."

"Oh, you pay them no mind. They are just jealous. You now have become competition."

"Competition? Competition for what?" Katrina didn't like being glared at.

"For the other young men in town, dear."

"Oh, they do not have anything to worry about. I have my eye on one particular man." Katrina had so much pride in her choice.

"You do? Well, do tell me, dear. Who has caught your eye?"

Katrina looked at her for a moment, not sure if she should reveal her feelings to anyone, but she knew she could trust Mrs. Jenkins. She had been a dear friend to her mother for many years.

"Well," Katrina blushed. "It is someone I have cared for for a long time."

"Go on," Mrs. Jenkins urged.

"You must not tell anyone."

Mrs. Jenkins crossed her heart.

"Okay, his name is Chad Miles. You know him. He has worked for our family for a while now."

"Katrina, I know exactly who you are referring to. He is a nice young man. Does he feel the same for you?"

"I am not sure. He kissed me once but told me I was like a little sister to him." Katrina looked down, a little depressed.

Mrs. Jenkins lifted Katrina's face up from under her chin. "Now you listen to me, child. You have all there is to offer a man and keep him happy. What matters is how you use it. Maybe he just needs to be reminded a little more often that you are a young woman and not that little tomboy running around anymore. He will come around."

Katrina smiled at her.

Mrs. Jenkins's face lit up. "I have just the thing." She was chattering all the way to the back of the store. "You know the Thorn's barn dance is in two weeks, and you must go. You will be the belle of the ball, or barn dance, for that matter." She giggled. Mrs. Jenkins came out of the back room carrying the most beautiful blue dress Katrina had ever seen. "You must try it on," she was insisting.

"Oh, I could not." Katrina was rubbing the material between her fingers. "I could never afford this. My mother would object."

"Oh, nonsense, child. This is a gift from me to you. A 'coming out of your tomboy' stage into the beautiful princess that you are."

Katrina blushed from the compliment. "Oh, Mrs. Jenkins, I do not know what to say."

"Say you will accept my gift and wear it to the dance. I will be proud to share with everyone you purchased it from my store. You in turn would be doing me a favor. I have wanted to bring in more yardage, and if others want prettier dresses for their daughters, then Mr. Jenkins will have to give in to my wishes of a bigger area to hold it all.

"I bought this dress from Sue Ellen Higgins, and she has more for me to buy and sell on consignment. So you see, by accepting the dress and being the prettiest belle at the ball, you will help me in return."

"I will do it." Katrina hugged the dress.

"Good, good. Now run along before it starts getting dark. The buckboard should be loaded with your supplies. I will put the items on your mother's tab."

Katrina gave Mrs. Jenkins a big hug. "Thank you so much."

"I will be thanking you soon. Now run along."

Mrs. Jenkins had a tear run down her check as she sent up a prayer to Katrina's father. "You raised her good. You would be so proud."

As Katrina climbed onto the buckboard, she felt a hand grip her wrist. She looked to see who had a hold of her; it was Hank Baxter. Katrina felt a chill run down her spine.

"Hi, Hank."

"Katrina, is that really you? In all my days, I would not have believed it. Robert was saying he saw a beautiful blonde he did not recognize go into the mercantile, and you know me. I have to know every woman in this town."

Katrina yanked her arm from Hank's grasp. "Look, Hank, I need to get going. Can we postpone this conversation for another time?"

"I do not think so." Hank started to climb up onto the buckboard.

Katrina did what came naturally for her, and she didn't care if she did make a spectacle of herself. She wasn't about to let Hank get the upper hand. She planted a foot on his right side and shoved as hard as she could then slapped the reins to get her team moving. Katrina righted herself and waved goodbye to Hank as he was dusting himself off while Robert stood there, laughing.

Katrina was feeling that maybe Chad had a good point, but then again, she knew how to take care of herself. On the other hand, she was glad Bo took it upon himself to escort her to town. So far, this had been a really good day. She was delighted to bring the news of the Thorn's barn dance, in two weeks, to the dinner table.

Katrina steered the wagon to the front of the house so it could be unloaded. No one was in sight. As she climbed down, her mom came onto the front porch, wiping her hands on her apron.

"Where is everyone, Mama?"

"Oh, I expect they are around her somewhere. Let's do what we can, and hopefully, someone will come around in the meantime."

The two of them worked about twenty minutes unloading and hauling groceries and supplies into the house; still no one had come around.

They finished what they could handle. The rest was too heavy.

"Mama, you find it strange we are the only two on this ranch?"

"It does seem strange. Where do you suppose everyone is?"

"I do not know, but I aim to find out. I will get some help for the heavier items."

"Okay, dear. I need to get back to preparing my supper. By the way, you sure look pretty, dear."

"Thanks, Mama." Katrina felt so warm from all the nice compliments she had received all day. "I will be in to help soon."

Katrina went into the barn. No one was there. She went to the bunkhouse, and no one was there. She went into the pasture and could hear some muffled men's voices coming from the other side of the outbuilding. She headed in that direction, trying not to get the bottom of her dress dirty. She should have changed. She would just as soon as she got a few men to help unload the buckboard.

Katrina walked around the building and came to a shocking halt.

"Silver Ghost!" she screamed. "What are you doing to him?" This was directed at Theo, who was holding the whip.

Katrina ran in front of Silver Ghost to protect him. As she turned, Theo knew there was going to be hell to pay. "I asked you a question, Theo. Who gave you orders to whip this man?"

Theo stammered, "James, Ms. Katrina."

Katrina could see Theo was confused. It was known that Theo had been thrown from a few too many bulls in his time, but he was a good man and did as he was told. She could tell he was only following orders and not acting out on his own.

"Have I done somethin' wrong Ms. Katrina? I do not want to do nothin' wrong." Theo looked like he was ready to cry.

Katrina felt bad for Theo, but now was not the time to be showing concern for him. "Where is James?" She snapped at one of the other men.

"I will go find him." Several of the other men chimed in at the same time as they scrambled off.

"What did this man do, Theo? Why is he being whipped?"

Theo just looked at her. He didn't have an answer.

Katrina turned to look at the damage that had been done to Silver Ghost's back. "Silver Ghost, I am so sorry," she cried openly, tears running down her cheeks.

She couldn't touch him. It seemed everywhere she went to touch was bloody. His back was nothing but mush. By the looks of it, the whip had struck him at least fifty times. Was he still alive? "Silver Ghost, can you hear me? Please do not be dead," she begged him. She was standing in front of him; she lifted his face with her hands as gently as she could.

His eyes opened. "Moonglow, I had to . . ." With this, his head dropped as he passed out.

"Help me get him down, Karl."

"Yes, ma'am." Karl cut the ropes, and Silver Ghost's body hit the dirt hard.

Karl and Katrina got him onto his stomach. Karl proceeded to cut the ropes from Silver Ghost's wrists.

"Please do not give up, Silver Ghost. Hang in there. I will get to the bottom of this. I promise."

She heard the men coming around the corner. She stood to face them, but not before she grabbed Karl's gun from his holster.

She had more anger in her than she had ever known possible.

Chad and Bo came up behind James. Neither of them was aware of the happenings, but one of the men thought they should be there for the confrontation.

"James, you better have a good reason for treating this man the way you just did!" she growled at him. Her hands were shaking; she had never pointed a gun at one of her brothers.

"He be an Indian," he casually remarked.

Katrina shot at the ground, just missing his right foot. "So?" she raged.

James jumped when the bullet hit the ground just inches from his foot. "What do you mean so? His kind killed our pa, or have you forgotten?" He yelled at her as he looked at the ground with disbelief where the bullet had barely missed his foot.

"Maybe some Indians but not his kind. His people have been friends with us for many, many years. He speaks English better than you or I do. His people were not the ones that killed our pa, and no I have not forgotten." All of a sudden, she felt really tired, but she bucked up. "You need to get your facts straight before you go around whipping people."

Chad watched to make sure things didn't get out of hand. He knew Katrina wouldn't shoot her own brother, but he had to admit she made him jump when she fired at James's foot. What he didn't like seeing was how she was standing up for this Indian against her own family. By the looks of things, she had some strong feelings for this Silver Ghost, and he didn't like it one bit.

James didn't care what Katrina said about the Indian. As far as he was concerned, they were all alike. "Stand aside, Katrina, he does not deserve to live. He tried to kidnap you."

"What?" She shot at his other foot. "I cannot believe you. If you plan on laying one more hand on him, you will have to go through me first." Katrina straightened her back and stood her ground.

Evelyn had heard the shots from the house and came running around the corner to hear James say, "Have it your way, sis." James started to move forward but was abruptly stopped by Chad's hand on his shoulder.

"Touch her, James, and I will personally rip you apart limb by limb." Chad didn't have to yell it. He simply stated it matter-of-factly.

James turned to face Chad. "Oh, Chad, you are not siding with that Indian, are you?" James whined.

"I am just stating a fact, James. I would suggest you not test my patience right now." Chad's eyes were locked with Katrina's while he spoke. They didn't waver until Silver Ghost moaned in pain, and then she went to Silver Ghost.

Chad had to question himself if he were crazy or not. If the Indian were dead, then she couldn't fall in love with him. Now it looked like she was going to be the Indian's caretaker in every way. Chad didn't like it, but it was what Katrina wanted, and he realized he would do anything for her, anything.

The men started to break up. Chad and Evelyn went to Katrina's side. He looked at the man's back. "It is going to take a lot of doctoring to get that back to heal, Trina." Chad's voice was quiet.

"I know, Chad. Thank you for standing up for him." She turned to look in Chad's eyes. "I will never forget it."

Chad knew it wasn't the Indian he was standing up for; it was her. But for some reason, he couldn't bring himself to tell her how he felt, but he did reply with "I did this for you, not him. Are we clear on that?"

Katrina nodded her understanding.

"I'll help you get him to a bed," Chad offered.

"Take him to the guest room in the main house," she requested.

"Do you think that is a good idea, Katrina?" Evelyn asked, worried.

"I will have it no other way, Mama," Katrina said, finishing any more talk about the subject.

They all headed for the house. Mrs. Holt had a thousand questions, but she would wait.

With the subject closed by Katrina's firm demand, Chad and one of the hands carefully carried the Indian to the guest room. They gently laid him on his stomach after Katrina pulled the covers back.

James was making a big stink about an Indian being in his house.

Bo didn't care for the whole situation either, but Katrina seemed to have things under control, so he told James to go bunk in the bunkhouse for the time being. James was hotter than coal, but he did as his elder brother told him.

"Mama, can you boil some water for me and get me some clean bandages?"

"Yes, yes, of course. Katrina, is this a good idea?" Her mother's voice had a lot of worry in it. She knew James would not let this blow over easy.

"Yes, Mama. Just trust me."

Katrina turned to Chad as he asked, "Do you want me to fetch Doc Brume, Trina?" He was talking in hushed tones.

"No, I know what to do. You have helped enough already." She put her hand on his shoulder then kissed his cheek. "Thanks again, Chad. I owe you one."

He smiled at her. "Just call it even, my little Trina." They looked into each other's eyes for a moment. She wanted him so badly to kiss her. She needed him to kiss her right now. She needed his strength. His lips just barely brushed hers.

Silver Ghost moaned. "You better tend to your patient," Chad whispered as he pulled away.

She watched him walk out of the room. She wanted to go after him, but Silver Ghost moaned again, so she went to him instead.

When Chad walked out of that room, he felt he had made the biggest mistake of his life. She would grow closer to that Indian day by day nursing him, and all Chad would be able to do was sit back and watch.

Chad walked back to the bunkhouse. The men had all kinds of questions, but Chad just kept walking straight through to his separate quarters and closed the door. He didn't have an appetite. He knew Mrs.

Holt had been slaving over the stove all day, but he just didn't think he could eat.

Sleep did not come easy for Chad. He kept seeing an angel in a pretty pink dress.

It was early the following morning. Katrina was applying salve to Silver Ghost's back. He had been restless all night. She could tell he wasn't aware of his surroundings. When he murmured, it was his Indian tongue he used.

After applying the salve, she sat on the chair she had pulled up to the bed the evening before. It was the one she had dozed off in several times while he lay quiet. She closed her eyes for just a moment.

Katrina jumped at the voice. She hadn't been aware anyone had come into the room.

"How is he doing?" Chad asked in a low voice.

"Oh, you startled me, Chad. How long have you been here?"

"Awhile" was all he said. He didn't tell her he had been watching her apply the salve, all along wanting to stop her from touching another man. He couldn't believe these feelings were getting so strong, stronger every day. What had she done to him all of a sudden? Before, he was hardly aware she was around. Now he knew her every move.

"Has any fever set in?" Chad broke the silence.

"No, not yet, but we are just beginning," she answered, worried.

"Well, if it does, you call for me. I will fetch a remedy from Doc Brume." Chad walked over and put his hands on Katrina's shoulders from behind, as she sat on the chair.

Chad massaged her shoulders for a minute. She was definitely stressed. "He is lucky to have you, Katrina," Chad whispered.

She reached up and cupped his hands then gave a little squeeze. "He has got to be okay, Chad. He just has to." Tears welled up in her eyes.

Chad felt sick. She obviously had fallen in love with the Indian. His hopes were crushed. He turned and left the room.

Katrina spent the next six days with hardly any sleep. Silver Ghost had developed a high fever.

Chad had done as promised and collected the remedy from Doc Brume, but it didn't seem to be helping.

Katrina had refused to leave his side. She wouldn't listen to reason. She had lost weight, and Mrs. Holt was getting very worried.

Katrina had to see him through this. His back was healing as best could be expected.

Katrina was resting on the chair. She ached all over, and she could definitely use a bath, but she was afraid to leave him.

Several times, her mind wandered to the kisses he had given her. She thought about the words he had whispered to her before she left him the last time. He had said he would take her. Was that why he came here?

She wondered for a moment what it would be like to be married to an Indian, and she couldn't even comprehend what that would be like. She belonged here, with her family, with Chad. Plus she would only marry for love, and she didn't love Silver Ghost.

She felt sorry for Silver Ghost but not love. Satisfied with her conclusion, she slept, exhausted, so much that she didn't come to when Chad shook her.

"Trina." There was no answer. He was going to tell her to go to bed but was glad she was in such a deep sleep. He knew she would have refused anyway.

Chad picked her up and cradled her in his arms. She was so light. She couldn't have lost that much weight in one week, but it sure felt like she was a feather in his arms. As he turned, he saw the reflection of him holding her in the mirror. She looked like a child, so small next to his big body.

Chad gently carried her to her bed and laid her ever so gently down. He didn't want to wake her. She snuggled right into her pillow with a smile on her lips.

Chad stood over her for a few minutes, taking in her beauty. Even with the dark sunken circles under her eyes, she was beautiful. How he wished he could kiss her, but he knew she had made her choice. Unfortunately, he wasn't the choice. He wished the feelings he had for her had surfaced earlier, before the Indian came into her life. Now it was too late.

That thought reminded him there was a patient in the other room that needed to be taken care of, and she wouldn't want him left alone.

Katrina woke suddenly. Looking around and seeing that she was in her bedroom, she had to wonder if she had been dreaming. She got out of bed and went to the guest room to confirm that this had all been a bad dream. No, it hadn't. There was Silver Ghost sitting up in bed with Chad keeping him company.

Silver Ghost smiled when he saw her. "Moonglow," he called, "come sit by me."

Katrina was a little hesitant, but she really wanted to have a look at his back. She was so glad he was going to pull through.

Chad watched as Silver Ghost raked her in with his eyes. Silver Ghost's eyes became lustful toward Katrina.

Chad was seeing red.

Katrina approached the bed and was talking to Silver Ghost, not even acknowledging Chad. "I see you have recovered some. I was hoping your fever would break, but I did not think you would be sitting up in just a few hours." Her eyes said it all as far as Chad was concerned.

Chad piped in, "It has been more than a few hours, Katrina, and you have been sleeping for forty-eight hours straight."

"What?" She was shocked. "That cannot be."

"I carried you to bed the night before last. I have checked on you off and on, and I did not have the heart to wake you." He could see she was getting flustered.

Chad held up his hand to stop her tirade. "Not to worry, Katrina. As you can see, your ma and I have taken good care of your patient."

With that, Katrina smiled broadly at Silver Ghost.

Chad took it to mean that she was glad for her friend and felt they would rather be alone, so he got up to leave. "Now that you are up and about, I have better things to do." He was so edgy all of a sudden. He walked to the door and turned to say goodbye, but he was already dismissed. He left with a heavy heart.

"Chad," Katrina turned to thank him not even a few seconds after he walked out. That was strange. She would have to thank him later.

"Silver Ghost, I am glad you are better. Let me see your back." He leaned forward for her to inspect. "It sure is healing nicely. Are you hungry?"

Silver Ghost wrapped his arms around her waist. "I am," he said as he pulled her down to his lap. Katrina put her hands on his chest to push away.

"Silver Ghost, what are you doing?" As sick as he had been, he was still so much stronger than her. She was losing the fight. Silver Ghost crushed her lips to his, and what surprised her was that there was no spark like she felt the first time. Chad had been right about Silver Ghost taking advantage of her emotions. She couldn't escape his grasp, so she grabbed the back of his head and pulled on his hair until he finally released her.

When she was on her feet next to the bed, she slapped him hard. "You have no right kissing me," she scolded.

Silver Ghost only chuckled. What was this? Playing hard to get? Well, that was okay with him. Silver Ghost always liked a challenge.

"Moonglow, I came here to take you back as my wife." His eyes were sparkling with laughter from her next words.

"Do not call me that. My name in Katrina. Who do you think you are? You think you can just come here and haul me off as your wife? Why, you have not even asked me." Her hands were on her hips, and she huffed as she scolded him. "You have a lot of nerve, Mr. Ghost."

Silver Ghost burst out laughing over the use of the formal name. No one had ever called him Mr. Anything.

"What is so funny?" Katrina was annoyed. He had no right laughing at her. He had no right assuming she wanted to be his wife; he had no right making decisions for her.

Silver Ghost slowly got out of the bed and sunk to the floor. She almost went to him. Katrina stood aside, watching him struggle to his knees. It was obvious he was still very weak. Eventually, he got on his knees and looked up at her.

Katrina all of a sudden realized what he was about to do. She looked on in horror.

"I believe this is a custom of yours." Katrina started to say something, but he went on without letting her interrupt. "I would ask for you to be my wife, Moonglow."

Silver Ghost was looking up at her with such hope in his eyes. Katrina still stood with her hands on her hips and slowly sunk into the chair. Her eyes filled with regret because he was serious, and she didn't want to hurt him, especially after all he'd been through just because of her.

"I do not know what to say, Silver Ghost," she whispered.

"You do not know?" Shock was registered all over his face. He knew any squaw in his camp would be honored to be his bride. What was her problem? This playing hard to get was getting tiring. "Okay, Moonglow. I will give you seven sunrises to make up your mind. Then I want an answer." He was agitated that she didn't jump at the chance, and his words were stern.

"Seven days. I do not need seven days." He thought she would change her mind, and she was trying to let him down gently. Well, no one was going to dictate to her that she didn't know her own mind. "Silver Ghost, I am not in love with you. I will not marry except for love. So there is your answer, and just in case you need it spelled out, the answer is *n-o*." Her words were just as stern as his. She got up to leave the room just as James came barreling in.

"Now that you have him healed, I want him out of this house," James bellowed.

"He will leave when I say. Now get out of here before I regret what will happen next." James didn't need a second warning by the fire that was in Katrina's eyes.

Katrina left the room and didn't stop to talk to anyone who had been outside of the bedroom in other parts of the house. They all had heard raised voices, so each one tried to question her as she exited each room with a huff, but she paid none of them any mind. She just kept marching right out the front door and straight into Chad's brick wall of a chest.

Chad and Bo had heard the yelling up at the main house and took off at a run. "Whoa." Chad steadied her with both hands on her shoulders. "Where are you off to in such a blind fury, little lady?" Katrina was looking down, so Chad gently cupped her chin and lifted her face to look him in the eye.

Katrina had tears pooled in her big blue eyes.

"What's this, Trina? What's wrong?" the concern in Chad's voice was her undoing.

Katrina burst into tears. "Oh, Chad."

"Shhh." Chad pulled her into his arms.

Bo went inside to see what all the ruckus was about.

Katrina felt chills run up her spine and started crying harder.

Chad held her closer. She felt so right in his arms. He didn't know what had upset her, but it must have been big for her to cry as hard as she was now. He rarely saw her cry.

Chad holding her made her feel safe, protected. She liked the security it brought her, but it wasn't to last.

Bo walked out onto the porch. "Katrina, are you okay?"

She pushed herself out of Chad's arms. "I need to go for a walk," she responded as she headed down the stairs.

Chad hollered after her, "Do you want someone to talk to, Trina?" He was very concerned about her.

"No!" she snapped. She just wanted men to leave her alone. She vowed to start wearing breeches again starting tomorrow. She didn't like all the emotions and attention that being a *little lady* brought on.

Katrina's walk turned into a run. She ran faster and faster and faster until her lungs burned. She ran until she couldn't run anymore, then she dropped to the ground. What was the matter with her? She never cried. She didn't know if it was the exhaustion because she truly was exhausted.

It was plain and simple. She didn't want to marry Silver Ghost, so why was she so upset? He would leave, and everything would be the same again. Or would it?

Chad had gone into the house determined to get to the bottom of Katrina's state of mind. His first stop was the guest room. Silver Ghost was looking out the window. When he turned from the window, he had amusement written all over his face.

"See something funny?" Chad asked sarcastically.

Silver Ghost straightened. "I've gotten under her skin." He was so smug.

Chad wanted to take him down. He crossed his arms over his chest to keep from reaching out and grabbing him. "I think you are confused. Do not mistake concern and human compassion for love." Chad walked over to look out the window. "So exactly why is she so upset?"

"I have asked her to be my wife. It would mean leaving home, and she would miss her family." Silver Ghost lied as he boasted.

Chad was floored to say the least. "Well, I am sure you will both be very happy." He could hardly choke the words out. He stiffened and turned to look Silver Ghost straight in the eye.

They were both big men, but Chad was two inches taller and about twenty pounds of muscle broader. Right now, he stood his ground and projected his words with every fiber of his body, "If I ever find out you have hurt her, I will personally track you down and make you pay for it. Do not ever do anything to her against her will, and remember she is a woman above all else."

Silver Ghost didn't like the threat in Chad's words, but he wasn't worried. Once he and Katrina were gone, Chad would have no say in her life. Silver Ghost straightened his spine, still not as tall as Chad, and he said, "Oh, I promise she will love me like no other." Then he thought to himself, even if it is hate, it will be like no other.

Now Chad was the one who needed to get away. Before he knew it, without any thought, he was saddling his horse, Streak. He mounted and took off for town as if he had a posse on his tail.

Katrina had been heading back to the house when she saw Chad riding like the wind. She stopped just to admire how graceful he was. *What a man*, she thought to herself. Then she caught herself and stomped her foot. "Damn men, I want no part of them."

She reached the house and went straight to the guest room. She had a few things to say to Silver Ghost, and she wanted to get it over with, but when she got there, he was asleep. She decided to take a hot bath. What she had to say could wait until later.

Once her bath was over, she was feeling a lot better, especially after she put on the men's pants and one of her brothers' shirts.

Katrina found her mother in the kitchen. "Ma, could I ask a favor of you?"

"Sure, honey." Katrina rarely asked anything of anyone. She was so independent; her mother knew it must be important.

"Could you help me to make some women's riding clothes? Something a little more feminine than these?" Katrina was pulling the pant legs out that were way too big.

"Of course, honey. We can go into town tomorrow and pick out some fabric. I'm glad to see you're taking some interest in your attire." Her mother didn't want to pry too much, but she had been concerned about Katrina and her mood swings lately. She had been trying to pay close attention to Katrina to see if she could figure out what she could do to help. So far, she was still unsure.

"I just felt there were too many men around here already." Evelyn winked at her daughter and smiled.

Katrina walked over to her mother and kissed her cheek. "Thanks, Mama."

Katrina headed for the guest room. She was surprised to see Silver Ghost reading a book when she stopped at the threshold.

He looked up as she stood there. "Hi, Moonglow." His face broke into a frown when he saw her clothes. "I like you much better in woman's clothes."

"Well, that is exactly why I am not wearing them," she huffed and then took a deep breath. "Silver Ghost, if I asked you to leave when you are well enough, would you?" she asked quietly.

"Well, that all depends," he answered, grinning sheepishly.

"On what?" She was starting to get her dander up again. He had a way of making her angry.

"On you, of course."

Katrina wanted to wipe that grin off his face. "What about me?"

"Would you be going with me?" He was still hopeful.

"No." It was short and to the point.

"No?" He was determined to take her with him.

"Silver Ghost, I already told you I would not marry you, and I meant it."

"Well, we will just see about that." She didn't know it, but he would force her to go with him whether she wanted to or not.

There was no talking to him, so she just turned and left.

CHAPTER SIX

Chad sat in the salon with his boots up on the table. He had been drinking heavy for the last two hours. This wasn't like him at all. If he did visit the salon, which was seldom, he knew his limit.

The salon girls kept taking their chances on changing his mind, wanting him to go upstairs for a little entertainment. Maureen was dying to get him alone for the evening. She'd been with him once before. It had been an evening she would never forget. Chad Miles was definitely a tender lover.

Maureen approached him. Her voice was husky, "Hi, honey. I have not seen you in my neck of the woods for a long time. Where you been hidin'?"

"Hiiii, doll. I beeeen a-a-around," he said. His words were slurring.

"You look like you are trying to drown something with that bottle in your hand." She hoped it wasn't a woman. She liked Chad. She'd give up her line of work for a man like him.

"Maybe, maaaybe not," he said matter-of-factly.

"Well, maybe I can help you forget all your troubles for the evening, Chad." When Maureen saw the expression on his face, she thought, *Then again, maybe not*. "Who is she, Chad?"

"Who is whooo?" He snapped his head up.

"The woman that is eating at your heart?"

"There isss nooo woman. All you wooomen are tha same. You think you knooow everthin'."

Maureen could see he had it bad for one lucky girl, even if he wasn't willing to admit it. He probably was like every other man and didn't even realize he had it bad for the girl. "Well, my offer still stands about going upstairs. What do you say, Chad?"

"I saaay not tooonight, dollll." Chad stood and attempted to leave but had to sit back down. He looked up at Maureen who had a know-it-all look on her face again. "Caaan ya put me ooon my horssse?"

Maureen wanted to laugh. He was so cute. "Chad, I do not know what your horse looks like." She was grasping at straws, trying to get him to stay.

"Nooo problemmm. Just helllp me to that doooor." He was pointing and swaying again. Whoa, he was seeing two doors.

Maureen immediately grabbed his arm and swung it over her shoulder. It was obvious he was determined to leave. "Okay, cowboy."

It was slow going. He had drunk more than his share and stumbled a couple of times. At the door, she looked at him. "What now, cowboy?"

Chad hollered "Streeeeak," and Maureen was surprised to see this beautiful horse approach them and nuzzle Chad's hand.

Chad never had to tie Streak. It was as if he and his horse were best friends.

Maureen had to help Chad get his foot in the stirrup. The horse waited patiently while they attempted three times to get Chad in the saddle.

One of the men entering the salon took pity on Maureen and threw Chad's other leg over the horse.

Chad looked down at Maureen and tilted his hat. "I'll beee seeeeing ya."

"Not if that woman has anything to say about it," she mumbled as she smacked his horse on the rump.

Katrina was in her bedroom. Her window had been left open on purpose. As long as she could remember, whenever Chad went out for the day, she would leave it open to make sure he came home safe. She could hear a rider from a distance. He was talking to someone. No, he was singing. She couldn't remember ever hearing Chad sing before, but it sounded like his voice.

She ran out onto the porch. Chad was swaying all over in his saddle. What kept him in the saddle, she didn't know, and the tune he was singing was awful. "Oh, Chad," she sighed. She grabbed Streak's reins and gave the horse a big hug. "Thanks, Streak, for bringing him home."

She went to help Chad off his horse. "Come on, you big lug. I'll put you to bed."

"Bessst offffer I evvver had." He winked at her. Katrina turned beet red.

Unfortunately, he was too big and came down with a thump. "Oh! Chad, are you okay?" She finally got him off the ground.

"Triinaa darrrlin', yooou're beautifulll. Why you outssside in yooour nightdressss?"

She smiled at him. "Oh, I just thought you might need help putting Streak away." She was leading him to the separate side door to his quarters in the bunkhouse. When inside, he plopped down on the bed.

Katrina pulled one boot off then the other. She started to unbutton his shirt, and he grabbed her hands. His face was so serious she was almost afraid of him.

Chad pulled her down to lie on top of him and kissed her. The kiss seemed almost desperate, and then he put his tongue in her mouth. At first, she was a little scared for fear he might not stop if she asked him to, then he gentled the kiss and was teasing her tongue with his. She started to play the same game, and he nibbled her bottom lip. He hadn't kissed her this way before—almost frantic—and she came to realize this was much more intimate.

He tasted of whiskey. He had his hands all tangled in her hair, holding her to him as if she were a lifeline. He moaned deep in his throat and pulled her even closer. This kiss sent shivers up her spine, and she found she didn't want it to stop.

When he finally pulled away, he buried his face into her neck and whispered, "Pleasse do not maarrry him."

Katrina's face broke out into a wide smile. She realized it was because of her that he was so drunk.

"Chad," she said. She started to tell him that she had already turned Silver Ghost down, but he engulfed her mouth with his before she could say more. Oh, she liked the way he was kissing her. The spark had not died with him as it had with Silver Ghost.

Katrina knew exactly when Chad had fallen asleep or passed out; she couldn't tell the difference. The kiss had gotten slower and slower. She just covered him up and sat at the edge of his bed for a moment. What a handsome man he was. He had such good qualities. The biggest of all was how much he gave and did for others. Her heart just swelled with the love she felt for him.

She kissed him gently on the forehead and whispered, "Sweet dreams."

Katrina went to Streak and led him into the barn. "What a good horse you are. I'm so glad he is home safely." She took off the saddle and brushed

Streak, talking to him the whole time, telling him how much she cared for his owner.

Katrina returned to her bedroom feeling warm inside. Love really didn't have to be a bad thing. She took out her diary and wrote,

> Dear Diary,
>> I think I am falling in love with
>> The most wonderful man.
>> I miss you, Pa. I love you, Pa.

Chad woke with a splitting headache. He couldn't remember much of last night. He couldn't even remember pulling his boots off and climbing into bed, but he must have because here he was sitting on the side of his bed with his boots on the floor.

He leaned over to pick up one of his boots and felt very dizzy. He was afraid he was going to be sick. He tugged one boot on then the other. This was going to be a very long day. "Damn," he swore and then cringed because it hurt to talk. As a matter of fact, it hurt to think, and think he must do because he knew he had tons to do.

He had fallen behind in his work taking care of Katrina's Indian for two days, but she needed the sleep, and he didn't have the heart to wake her.

Chad slowly walked outside. The sun hurt his eyes. It took him longer than normal for his eyes to adjust. Oh, this was going to be a long day. He didn't even know what time it was.

It dawned on him that Streak was probably around here somewhere with his saddle still on.

Chad walked into the barn to see Streak all taken care of. He couldn't remember if he put him away last night or not.

Slowly Chad made his way to the kitchen in the main house.

Katrina looked up and laughed. "You look like you had a good time last night, Chad."

He covered his ears and whispered, "Do not talk so loud." Everyone at the table burst out laughing. Chad shot them a killing look, which only made them laugh harder.

"You sit down, Chad, I will get you a cup of coffee," Katrina was quick to offer.

"Straight black, please. I think I need a whole pot." He had eye contact with Katrina. She was so pretty, and when she smiled at him like that, it warmed his insides.

Silver Ghost, standing on the sidelines, broke the trance that seemed to have developed between the two of them by clearing his throat quite loudly. He didn't like what he saw developing between those two. He decided right then and there to put his plan into action right away.

As soon as breakfast was over, Chad gathered all the hands to give orders for the day. "We need to round up the last of the stray cattle and their calves and finish branding. There should be close to two hundred, give or take a few, that still need branding. Divide yourselves into groups of four and bring them in. We should get them branded within a couple of days."

The men started breaking up. Chad headed back to his quarters to grab a bandanna. When he walked around the building, he saw the Indian kissing Katrina. He didn't stick around. He wanted to choke the guy. His head was pounding, and his body felt like he had been run over in a stampede. The last thing he needed to do today was pick a fight he didn't think he could come out of on top.

If he had stuck around, he would have seen Silver Ghost rubbing his cheek asking Katrina, "Why did you hit me?"

Katrina was shooting daggers at Silver Ghost. "I told you to never kiss me again." And she stomped on his foot with the heel of her boot to make sure it hurt. Then she left him to hop around on one foot while she entered the barn.

Chad was just finishing up saddling Streak when Katrina walked in. He didn't say anything to her at first. He just watched her go get her saddle and proceed to saddle her horse.

"Where do you think you are off to this morning?" he asked, irritated.

"Why, out to round up the cattle. Ma and I were going to go into town, but that can wait until tomorrow," she offered.

"I do not think so," he grunted.

"Yes, it can. We were not after anything important," she said. She was obviously confused by his statement.

"No! I mean I do not think you are going to help round up the cattle—"

"What?" she cut him off. "And why not? I have always helped out on the range, and I do not intend to stop now." She was gaping at him.

He didn't know why he was trying to pick a fight with her. If truth be told, he would rather have her out there with him than here with that

Indian. "Women belong in the kitchen, not on the range." Whoa, he knew he crossed the line, but he wanted to hurt her the way she was hurting him.

"Well, of all the nerve, Chad Miles. I have never been more insulted. Nothing has changed in the last couple of weeks."

Chad walked over and put his hands on her shoulders, but she jerked away. "Get your hands off me. I have no intentions of being left out on my own ranch, and you have no right trying to keep me from what I enjoy most." She was very angry now.

"Oh, yes, I do. I run the show around here, and you know it. Your ma put me in complete charge. So that gives me every right." He was annoyed with her attitude. Why couldn't she be a typical woman?

Katrina was fuming now, "Well, you could lose those rights. You are not so invincible, you know." She regretted the words just as soon as she said them. She knew no one would do as good a job as he did, but she wasn't about to let him start pushing her around now. He never tried in the past; she couldn't figure out why he would start now.

She couldn't believe she had thought she was falling in love with this chauvinistic fool.

"Ya, well, just try to replace me then. I will not have any problems finding work someplace else." With those words, he mounted Streak and headed for town.

Katrina stood there numb. He wasn't really leaving, was he? How did this get so out of hand? Who did he think he was anyway? Nobody was going to tell her what to do. She was going out with the men just as she always had, and she would show him.

The day had been backbreaking. Katrina had never worked so hard in her life. She had taken her anger for Chad out on her horse, Trader. How dare he try to change her and keep her from doing all the things she loved most! This ranch was her life, and no one was going to tell her differently. "In the kitchen? In the kitchen? Of all the nerve!"

The argument with him proved to her that more than anything, she hated the idea of ever settling down just to have some man tell her what she was or wasn't allowed to do. No man was going to tie her down, ever.

It was almost dusk. Bo had taken over Chad's job for the day. He had no idea where that fool had gone. He wasn't sure what had taken place between Chad and Katrina, but he aimed to find out.

Bo hollered out to all in earshot, "Head in for supper, men"—he stopped and looked at Katrina—"and woman. Ma's probably waiting on us." Bo caught Katrina's eye again. "I would like a word with you."

Katrina waited as Bo reined his horse up next to hers. They both dismounted and walked their horses. Bo asked her, "Do you happen to know where Chad was today?" There was a long silence. "Well?"

Katrina didn't know where to start. She wasn't so sure she understood it herself. Then she blurted out, "Chad must have gotten the wrong impression in our conversation earlier."

"And what impression would that be?" He raised his eyebrows at her.

"I think he thinks I fired him." Katrina shrugged then instantly shied away when he hollered at her.

"What?"

"Well, our conversation kind of got heated. I did not come right out and tell him he was fired. I just told him he was not irreplaceable, then he left." Katrina squared her shoulders. She was proud she stood up to him.

"Katrina, sometimes you do not know when to stop with your insults. Chad has been good for us. He has pulled us through a lot of hardships with his common sense and knowledge. It is not that I have not learned from him and could not run the place. It is that he has become a part of this family. He is like an older brother to me, and I have a lot of respect for the man. If I did not know better, I would say he thinks of us as family too."

Katrina knew everything he said was true. "I am sorry, Bo. I just do not want anyone, whether it is a man or woman, telling me what I can or cannot do. He was acting like he is my keeper, and I do not want to be kept by anyone. I want to think for myself. If I make mistakes, I have no one to answer to but myself. There is no reason I should not be out here on this range helping. I can shoot better than all the men except for you and Chad, and I ride just as well, so when he told me I should be in the kitchen, I came unstrung."

Ouch, that had to have been one hell of a conversation. Bo couldn't help but smile to himself. He could picture Katrina's face when Chad threw that at her.

Katrina was still talking, "I have proven myself over and over out here. Like the time that loco bull was charging Britt. Three of you men shot and missed. I got that bull right between the eyes on my first shot. And then the time—"

Bo cut her off, "You do not have to convince me that you can hold your own, sis. I know you can. I just cannot believe Chad was trying to put apron strings on you. He knows as well as anyone you are capable of doing this work."

Katrina's face broadened with a big smile as she cut him off. "Why, thank you, Bo. That was very nice of you to say."

"Ya, well, do not let it go to your head." He winked at her. "I will ride into town when we finish supper and find him."

They mounted their rides and rode into the compound shortly after that. Evelyn met them on the porch. "Bo, do you know why Chad would have come to collect all his gear?" The worry lines were deep on her forehead.

Bo looked at Katrina, who had a sorry expression on her face, then back to his mom, "Ya, Ma, I do. I will get him to stay. Do not worry. It is nothing that cannot be fixed."

They both dismounted, and Bo smacked Katrina on the rump then pushed her toward the house. "Go put on your apron."

"Ouch!" She turned and glared at him, then he winked at her, and she started to laugh.

"Bo, Chad is out in the bunkhouse right now, packing. You will talk to him now?" Evelyn pleaded.

"Good. That will save me a trip to town tonight. I am a little beat."

Bo turned toward the bunkhouse. Evelyn went into the house, while Katrina was worried on the porch for a minute then decided to put the horses away.

Earlier that morning, Chad had ridden into town after his and Katrina's argument.

He knew she didn't fire him, but he couldn't stand watching her being pawed by another man, let alone that Indian.

Their argument was just the icing on the cake. He knew she could handle herself on the range, and it probably would have been better for her to be out there with him, where he could keep an eye on her, versus at the house with her hot-blooded friend.

Chad was losing his head over her. She was driving him crazy, so much so that he wasn't thinking straight anymore.

Chad tied his horse off in front of Barbara's boarding house. Her place was the cleanest in town that rented rooms.

"Well, hi, Chad." Barbara was standing in the doorway, wiping her hands on her apron.

Chad had forgotten what a beauty she was. She stood five foot six inches with auburn hair down to her waist. Her complexion was clear, not a single freckle on her face. She still spoke with a bit of an Irish accent, although she had lived here in the States for over ten years now. And that smile would warm any man's blood, but those green eyes were her most beautiful feature. The sparkle made you wonder what mischief she was dreaming up.

"Well, come into me place and let me take yer hat."

Chad wasn't sure why she was still a single woman. She had everything to offer any decent man. She was a real woman. She did all the things a woman should: sew, clean, cook, and give teas. Chad could smell something with a cinnamon scent baking in the oven now.

Barbara took him by the hand into her parlor. "Can I offer ye some coffee, Chad? I have a fresh pot on the stove."

"Why, that sounds mighty good, Barbara. Thank you." He watched her as she left the room. He decided he might just like staying here after all. It would help get his mind off that spitfire on the ranch.

These two were completely different women. One cut from silk and lace, the other from denim and rawhide.

Barbara returned with the tray of coffee. "Would there be a reason I'd be blessed by ye company this morning, Chad?"

"Yes, I was hoping you had a room unoccupied." His fingers were crossed.

"Well, as a matter of fact, I do. But why would ye be looking for a room?" She knew the Holt family depended on him.

"Well, just say it is personal and leave it at that." He was trying to be polite, plus he didn't want it going around that he had feelings for a spitfire that chose an Indian over him. Although he hadn't really let her know his feelings, people wouldn't see it that way. They'd just look at the outcome.

"Okay, Chad. I won't be a prying. I'll just show ye the room ye will be occupying. The last man, he just left last night. It's all cleaned for ye." Barbara stood to lead him to a comfortable room. "My room is right there." She pointed across the hall. "If ye be needing anything in the night."

Barbara saw him blush and couldn't help but smile. She was a decent woman and would never fool with any of her tenants. After all, she had a reputation to uphold, but Chad Miles was a different story. She had had her eye on him for a very long time.

"Where's ye gear, Chad?" *He was a curious one*, she thought.

"I will fetch it in a while. I needed to know where I would be hanging my hat before I packed."

After coffee and cookies, Chad had ridden out to a couple of different ranches, and as he expected, he could have his pick. He told them he would let them know in a week where he wanted to settle.

The whole time, his heart was heavy. He knew he would miss the entire Holt family. They were like family to him.

He needed to head out to the ranch and get his gear. He knew he would be hitting the ranch about the same time the men would be coming in off the range. He wanted to let Bo know what was happening. He felt he owed it to him.

Chad knew Bo could run the place just fine, and if he had any problems, Chad would make sure Bo knew where to call on him.

Now Chad was in the bunkhouse stuffing the last of his belongings into a cloth sack.

Bo entered and asked, "Chad, what gives—" Bo was surprised to see Chad really packing.

"I will be honest with you, Bo. Your sister is driving me nuts."

"What do you mean? If you are talking about your argument this morning, she told me all about it. She said she did not really fire you. Is that what has brought all this on?"

"Bo, you have to give me your word that this conversation will not go any further than us."

"Well—" Bo started to say.

Chad cut him off. "Give it!" he ordered.

"Okay, okay." Bo put his hands up to ward off the harshness of Chad's demand. "Chad, you have my word. Now what has got you in such a huff?"

"Did you know your sister is going to marry that Indian?" Just by Bo's expression, Chad knew he was shocked.

"Over my dead body," Bo spat.

"Well, he told me himself." Chad's face creased as if he were in deep pain.

"I do not believe it, not one word of it. Why, she just told me today she did not want anyone telling her what she could or could not do." Bo was quiet for a second, trying to think. "Chad, what does this have to do with you leaving?"

"I cannot handle it. I have always looked at your sister as a little sister myself, but lately, she has looked more like a woman to me, and I am not just talking about when she is wearing a dress. Damn it. And seeing that Indian kissing on her makes me go nuts." Chad's voice was rising again.

"Why, Chad, if I did not know better, I would say you were jealous." Bo was smiling. The thought of Chad being a real brother by marrying into the family was a pleasing thought.

"Ya, well, maybe I am, but I am also not fool enough to sit around and watch him paw all over her. I will be leaving until after they're married and gone."

"You mean you are going to be a coward and back down? Are you afraid of a little competition?" Bo pushed Chad in the chest. "What is the matter with you? If anyone can change her mind, it is you. You do not want her marrying him, do you?"

"No, of course not, but I am not going to stick around and get kicked in the gut every time I see them look at each other." Chad paced back and forth then continued, "Bo, you will do just fine for the ranch. You have learned all there is to know. I will be working out at the Miller's ranch if you need me for anything. Please tell your ma I had to move on for now. I would tell her myself, but I do not even want to get into it with your sister again. I will come by in a few weeks to see your ma again, once things have settled down." Chad turned to face Bo and shake his hand. It wasn't enough. Chad pulled Bo into a bear hug. "I will miss all of you." Then Chad pushed Bo away, grabbed his bag, and walked out.

Chad walked to the front of the barn and was tying his gear onto the back of his saddle. Katrina was just exiting the barn from putting the horses in their stalls. Chad had hoped to get on his way without running into her. He didn't want another argument. He didn't know what to say, so he waited and let her speak first.

Katrina had all kinds of emotions running through her when she saw Chad with his gear. If only she could tell him how she felt without making a fool of herself.

"Chad, I am sorry about this morning. I did not mean to make you think you were fired. That is not what I meant at all." She was shaking inside now for fear he was really going to leave. What would she do without him?

She was so naturally beautiful. He wanted to reach out and pull her into his arms, but he refrained. "Trina, I know what you said. I am leaving for other reasons."

"What then, Chad? At least be honest with us. Is there something we could help you with?"

Oh, if she only knew. She could not marry Silver Ghost. That would settle everything. But he couldn't voice that.

"No, Trina, it is something I have to work out on my own. I hope I will see you around sometime."

Katrina had tears welling up in her eyes now. She fought them hard. She didn't want to seem like a child in his eyes. She ran into his arms and barely whispered, "I am going to miss you."

Holding her was killing him, but he couldn't have let her go if he tried. He wanted so bad to take her with him, but she didn't belong to him.

Behind the screen of the porch, Silver Ghost had been watching the two of them. He couldn't hear their conversation. He just knew Katrina in Chad's arms was not going to continue. Silver Ghost walked out onto the porch and slammed the screen door.

Both Chad and Katrina jumped to separate themselves. Chad felt the emptiness immediately. "There is your patient," Chad said to Katrina. Then just to spite that Indian, he pulled Katrina to him again and kissed her with all the force he could without hurting her.

Katrina wrapped her arms around Chad's neck. She didn't want him to stop, but as quickly as he pulled her into his arms, he pushed her away and mounted his horse.

Before she could blink, he was gone. Silver Ghost was there with his hand holding her elbow, pulling her into the house. "Good rid . . . dens," Silver Ghost breathed. He was glad the guy was gone.

Katrina yanked her arm out of his grasp and told him, "Do not touch me."

"It is time for supper, Katrina," her mother was saying.

"I am not hungry, Ma. I will just take my iced tea to my room with me."

Evelyn knew Katrina was upset. "Okay, Katrina, but you have had a long, hard day. Are you sure you do not want to eat something?"

"No, Ma, just the iced tea."

Chad slowed down once he was out of sight. The heaviness of this decision was almost unbearable. Chad kept going over the night's conversation. Bo's words about him being a coward echoed in his ears over and over again. "I am not a coward!" he yelled. "I am a fool." Then he said more quietly, "Because only fools fall in love." He was an idiot. It wasn't love. It wasn't jealousy. She was just a kid. He couldn't figure out why he hadn't learned the first time that women were nothing but trouble.

Katrina went to her room and set her iced tea on the nightstand. She sipped it a couple of times and then downed it. She hadn't known she was so thirsty.

She had never felt so empty in her life, not even when she lost her father. This was different though. She was losing the one man she had been in love with for as long as she could remember. This wasn't just a little-girl crush as it had been in the past. This was for real.

She wasn't experienced enough to know all that was going on between them. She only knew he thought of her as a little girl. "I do not want to be your little sister!" she cried out loud.

Katrina sat up in bed and took out her diary, then she wrote.

> I do not want to be your little sister.
> Chad, I want to be your wife.
> I miss you, Pa. I love you, Pa.

Then she drew a heart with Chad's and her name in it. Then she proceeded to draw a jagged line across the middle to show her heart was broken. Her eyelids felt so heavy; she lay on her bed and cried.

Exhausted from what seemed like hours of crying, she finally slept. She had cried until no more tears would come.

Silver Ghost had seen the herb in Mrs. Holt's garden the day before and knew it would help in his plans. At dinner that evening, it wasn't hard to slip the herb into Katrina's tea.

Katrina felt herself floating in her dream. Then she was riding a horse. She was leaning against Chad's chest. She was snuggling next to him and could feel him stroking her hair.

His lips came to hers, and they were tender, but something was different. Katrina opened her eyes. She blinked a couple of times before she realized it was Silver Ghost's face she was seeing. The smile in his eyes was what caused her to break the kiss.

Katrina pushed away and almost fell off the horse. *Horse? Why am I on a horse, and how did I get here?* she wondered. She turned to look at Silver Ghost. He still wore that smug smile. She broke the silence, "Silver Ghost, where are we going?" She tried to sound very calm.

"To be with my people," he said. He was so casual about it.

"And why would I want to go be with your people?" Her voice was a little shaky.

"To be my wife of course."

"Of course," she repeated calmly, then she was shouting, "Of course? What do you mean to be your wife? I never agreed to this." She started to struggle, but his grip tightened. "Silver Ghost, you cannot do this. I do not love you. I already told you this."

"Oh, yes, I can, and I will. I told you the reason I came to your place was to make you my wife. I do not go back on my word."

"You have to stop. You have to let me go." This had gotten out of hand.

"You are not the kind of woman I want to let go of. I knew it from the moment I met you. I admit, at first, I thought of giving you to my brother, but once your true colors came out, I knew you were for me. That is why I came to get you. I know you said no when I asked you to marry me. You said it was because you did not love me. Well, I am going to help you to love me. You will see."

She cut him off, totally angry at his gall, "No, I will not, Silver Ghost. I am already in love with someone, and no matter what you do or say, you cannot change my feelings."

He was angry at her words. She could tell by how his body tensed when he spoke. "You will see. Now I will have no more talk on the subject." He kicked the horse to pick up speed. "We will set up camp in a couple of hours, then I will take you as my wife." He could feel her body stiffen. "My grandfather will marry us when we get to my people's camp."

Katrina felt a fear she had really never felt before. She didn't say anything for a while. She was beginning to think she was dealing with a madman, and she didn't want to push him over the edge.

This wasn't how she dreamed things would turn out. As a girl, she thought she would have a big wedding. All her family and friends would be there. Practically the whole town would attend too. Her daddy would give her away. She would wear a beautiful gown. It was one of the only times she had ever thought she would wear a dress, until recently, but most importantly, she would be marrying for love.

She knew she didn't love Silver Ghost. She might have been a little infatuated with him at first, but she knew her heart had belonged to Chad forever. "Oh, Chad I need you again," she silently prayed. She also prayed something would happen between now and tonight. She had to think.

"Silver Ghost?"

"Hum." He was very relaxed, looking forward to what was to come.

"I do not know how it is with your people, but my people believe in the marriage ceremony before they bed together. It is called consummating."

She was trying to buy a little time, and he knew it.

She went on, "My God also believes that a couple should wait until they are married before bedding. Can I ask this of you?"

Well, that did it. She said the right thing to buy herself a little time, but he was going to get her word. He knew how his people believed also, and bedding should wait until the vows are spoken.

"You mean to tell me that once we are married, you will submit yourself to me willingly?"

"Yes," she croaked out, praying that she could escape him before they reached his people's camp.

"Moonglow, I would have your word."

She wanted to throw up. She was one who believed one's word was what made a person. They were either honest, or they were not. She never had much tolerance for someone who would break his or her word.

"I promise." She shivered as she spoke those words.

"Moonglow, you will have your wish, as I also will have mine. As soon as we get to my people's camp, we will be married, and I will have you." He could feel her go rigid again. "I promise I will be a gentle lover, Moonglow." He nuzzled his nose into the long hair at the nape of her neck. "And you will want me as much as I want you."

Never, Katrina thought to herself, *and if I can help it, we'll never make it to your camp.* She was scared to death and knew she had to escape. It couldn't be that hard, especially with it one against one. She would try while he slept tonight.

CHAPTER SEVEN

"Bo," Evelyn called.

"Ya, Ma," he hollered from the den where he was looking over last week's town paper.

"Do you know where your sister is? I have been looking for her all morning."

"She and Silver Ghost left before daylight, Ma," he said, not completely in the conversation.

"Left where?"

"I do not know, Ma."

"Did you talk to her?"

"No, Ma. They were busy kissin'. I did not want to interrupt. Chad told me that they was gettin' hitched."

"What?" her tone echoed his when he had found out. She obviously didn't know anything either.

What Bo hadn't known was when Silver Ghost had heard Bo approaching this morning, he had sat down and wrapped Katrina's arms around his neck and pretended to kiss her. Lucky for Silver Ghost, the herbs were still working, and she hadn't woken.

"I do not believe she would want to marry, Silver Ghost. She spent a good part of the night cryin' after Chad left. I even thought there might be a relationship developin' there."

"Well, I know for a fact why Chad left, Ma."

"Why, Bo? Did somethin' happen I should be knowin' about?"

"He made me give my word, Ma."

Evelyn knew they had raised their children to be honorable, and keeping someone's secret was something they were taught at a young age. She left it at that.

"Well, I will ask your sister about it when she gets back. If you see her before I do, let her know I want to talk to her. I want to know about this marriage business. Just 'cause your pa's gone doesn't mean we don't stick to formality 'round here."

"Yes, Ma." The whole thing annoyed Bo. He didn't want his sister marrying the Indian. The fact that his father was killed by the likes of him was too much to digest.

Katrina sat watching the flames of the fire. She had really thought that Bo or someone would come looking for her by now.

It had been four days since they had left the ranch. As the flames danced, she was wondering what she could try next to escape. She hated him. He had no right to take her away from her family. She just wanted to go home.

Every attempt to escape had failed. Silver Ghost was just too alert. The first night, she had walked away as quietly as she could. She knew he was asleep and was certain she hadn't made a sound, but he had tackled her from behind, not even three hundred yards out of the camp spot. He had rolled her over, and then he proceeded to kiss her so seductively she was afraid it wasn't going to end with the kiss. His hands were traveling up and down her body, and when he cupped her breast, she bit his lip.

Silver Ghost pulled away with a smile and told her in no uncertain terms that her punishment would be more severe if she tried to escape again.

The second time, she had tried tying him up in his sleep. She frowned as she thought of her own stupidity of tying his feet first. To think she was dumb enough to believe he would still be asleep when she got to his hands. He had waited for her to get to his hands then took her by surprise.

He was all over her. She shuddered, remembering the look in his eyes. She was certain he was going to rape her. In a way, his feet being tied helped because he came to his senses while untying the rope.

Ever since that night, which was two nights ago, he'd tied her up to him while they slept. She knew she had brought this all on herself, yet she couldn't help but hate him for what lay ahead for her.

Silver Ghost was watching her as she sat by the fire. "What are you thinking, Moonglow?" Although he spoke softly, she jumped when he startled her from her thoughts. He couldn't believe how many different expressions went across her face in such a short time. She was so transparent when it came to her feelings. Her expressions showed it all: hurt, disappointment, worry, fear, happiness, and love, which was the last emotion he had seen when she looked at Chad. He knew he could change that for her. He would make her forget Chad and fall in love with him. She would see.

When she didn't answer, he walked over to her. "I asked you a question, Moonglow!" His voice was gentle as he sat down beside her.

"I was thinking of home," she lied. She couldn't tell him she was plotting another escape. She had almost come to the conclusion that the only way she would ever really escape would be to kill him, and she didn't think she could do that.

"You do not need to think of there anymore. You will have a new home, a husband to care for, children to tend to, duties as a chief's wife—" he was going to go on, but she interrupted.

"A chief's wife? You didn't tell me you were the chief. Should you be away from your people so much?"

He could tell she was shocked. He had to laugh, hoping that she was impressed. "Up until now, I have not had much reason to stay in camp. I have always been one to wander. I hunt alone most of the time. I like to keep a lookout. I am usually not too far from them, and they know it. Usually, my little brother can find me if someone needs me. Going to get you was the farthest I have been away in a long time."

"What do you mean up until now?" she asked.

"You will be a good reason to stay in camp. I will need to keep you warm at night, plus we will want to have lots of children, and I cannot plant any seeds if I am not bedding with you."

Katrina felt the heat rise in her cheeks. Silver Ghost broke into a roaring laugh.

"What is so funny?"

"You are so innocent when it comes to bedding, but you will have a good teacher. Do not worry." He was still laughing but stopped abruptly with her next words.

"You think mighty highly of yourself. I do not want to be taught anything by you. Can you not get that into your thick skull?" she huffed then stood and walked away.

He knew she wouldn't go far. She was too afraid that he would take her. He almost did the last time she tried to escape. He remembered how he had wanted her so badly. He could see the terror in her eyes though. He didn't want her that way. He wanted it to be a mutual agreement. Why was she so damned stubborn?

He had a lot to offer her. He knew she wasn't playing hard to get anymore. He could tell by her expressions that she hated him, not because he was an Indian but because she loved another and was taken from him. Time would heal her though.

He knew that he could get her to love him once they were back with his people, and if it couldn't be love, at least she would learn to respect and honor him. Then maybe, just maybe, love could follow. If not, then they would at least have children together and love those children dearly. The children would give them a common bond. He would protect her with his life, share with her, honor and respect her. He would make her have no other choice but to fall in love with the father of her children.

Then it hit him. One needed to earn love and respect. He needed to make her feel special. He needed to court her, give her gifts, and learn her likes and dislikes. This decided, he would start tomorrow.

He was relieved to see her walk back into camp about half an hour later. He was starting to get a little anxious. He didn't want to have to hunt her down again. "I am glad to see you are back."

"I just bet you are. I am surprised you were not out looking for me," she stated coolly.

"Well, I knew you would not go far. You see, there is no place you could go to hide from me. I would find you no matter what. Then I would have my way with you."

"Do not threaten me," she snapped. Boy, how she wished she had the courage to have kept walking. She had been so tempted.

"Oh, that is not a threat, Moonglow. It is a vow, and I never break my word." He could tell he struck a nerve and was sorry, but she had to know he would never let her go, never!

Katrina stomped over and lay on the blanket they had been sharing each night. She was always so uncomfortable. There was nothing for her head to rest on since he had started tying her up at night. She wished she were home in the comfort of her own bed. Her ma must be worried sick over her disappearing.

Silver Ghost stoked the fire one last time before they turned in. He went to lie beside her. She lay there for a few minutes before asking, "You going to tie my hands and feet already? I am tired and want to go to sleep."

"Not tonight, Moonglow." He rolled her over to face him.

"Why? You cannot trust me," she spit out sarcastically. "What game are you playing now?"

"No games, Moonglow." He took her in his arms and started kissing her. She was so rigid and was pushing on his chest. He wanted her to relax, so he gentled and slowed the kiss.

His kiss became warm. It wasn't rushed or hard like it had been in the past. Fighting him was useless. His next move made her uncomfortable. He parted her lips and started exploring her mouth. She tried to pull away, but he had her snug tight. She only wanted Chad to kiss her this intimately.

He could tell the kiss was getting out of control for him. He wanted much more of her but couldn't. Not just yet. He pulled away. She was still pushing on his chest. She had that scared look again. He was going to have to take it good and slow with her. "I almost wish you would try to escape again, Moonglow. You are killing me with the need I have for you." His words didn't go over well. "Good night, Moonglow," he said as he rolled her over and pulled her up against him.

Katrina could feel his erection against her buttocks. She wiggled, trying to not touch him there, but it only made him harder.

Silver Ghost pulled her tighter against him and grunted, "Stop your moving. You are driving me wild." The nights were getting colder, and they needed each other's body heat. Otherwise, he would have rolled away from her.

That was it? He was just going to kiss her? Not take things further? She could feel his arousal against her back. She felt relief he didn't try to go further. She couldn't believe he really wasn't going to tie her up. Well, he would regret that when morning came and she was gone.

They both lay there for a long time in their own thoughts. She thought he would never go to sleep.

He wasn't about to fall asleep before her tonight. He wanted to show her he trusted her—at least let her think he did—but he was no fool. He knew she was a pretty sound sleeper once she was out. His chances of her sticking around until morning were better once she was asleep.

Sleep finally took her. He pulled her even closer into the crook of his arm. Surprisingly enough, she nestled right in and didn't wake.

The following morning, Katrina woke with a feeling of dread. She sat up and couldn't believe she had fallen asleep. Silver Ghost was already up starting on a rabbit for breakfast.

"Sorry, I did not mean to wake you. Are you hungry?" He could tell she was mad.

She was so angry with herself for falling asleep. He had trusted her, and it worked. He played a trick on her; she just knew it. This was not how her morning was supposed to be. She hand blown her chance.

"No, I am not hungry," she snapped as she got up and folded the blanket.

He walked up behind her as she finished folding the blanket and reached around her to give her a bouquet of wildflowers.

No one had ever given her flowers before. Why did the first person have to be Silver Ghost? Tears were welling up in her eyes. She hated it when she got tears in her eyes. What was her problem lately? It seemed every time she turned around, she was starting to cry over something. She never used to cry.

"For you," he said.

She didn't take the flowers, so Silver Ghost turned her around to look at her. When he saw the tears, he was confused and angry. "Damn it all. What did I do now?" He took the bouquet and threw it down. "I was only trying to be nice. Let you know that there is a warm side to me too."

She knew that warm side. She felt it in his kiss last night. Something about that kiss made her want to escape even more than before. She didn't want to like it. She was beginning to wonder if she should just accept her destiny. This whole situation wasn't right. She didn't want anything from him except her freedom.

He was getting angrier with himself every day. Why he even bothered, he didn't know. Yes, he did. He had fallen in love with her. She had spunk and was tender, smart, tough, protective of her things, and beautiful. He had fallen in love with the side of her that was gentle and giving, loving and pure. She had a lot to offer. He only wanted a little of it.

They both went about their own business until he announced breakfast. She sat down but barely touched her food. "Better eat. We will travel for two sunsets before we stop for sleep."

"Why?" she barked.

How could he tell her that it would take that long before they reached his people, and he didn't want to take any more chances with her. She still wanted to escape, but that wasn't his biggest concern. He didn't want to put himself through another night of wanting her as bad as he had last night.

When he had woke this morning, he felt a need to take her. The need was so strong he almost couldn't suppress it. Once they were married, he wouldn't have to worry about that. She had given her word to submit to him willingly. That would be the turning point of their relationship and her feelings toward him.

"We will be with my people by the sunset of tomorrow. I do not want to waste any more time." He put it flatly so she would not question his word.

He could tell by her frown that her mind was racing trying to figure out how to get away from him. *Let her try,* he thought. Then she'll have to submit. He had let her know that his way with her would be the penalty if she tried to escape again. In a way, it would be better to get the whole ordeal over with so he could release the aching he had had ever since he had met her.

Oh, how sweet it will be.

This time, it was Katrina studying his facial expressions. She broke his train of thought, "What were you thinking just now?"

"You want the truth?" he asked mischievously.

She knew she was going to regret it, but she answered anyway, "Of course." His smile alone got her blushing.

"I was thinking of how sweet it is going to be to bed with you."

Katrina felt sick. At least he said *with.* He was still determined that the bedding was going to be a joint venture. He was crazy as far as she was concerned. She would never give into him.

"Would you rape me if I was not willing?" her voice was trembling.

This made him angry. "Have I yet?"

"No," she whispered.

"Believe me, Moonglow, when we do bed together, you will give me your permission. I have agreed to wait until the vows of marriage are said, and you have agreed to consummate the marriage. Or are you going to make a liar of yourself?" His temper was flying.

"No, my word like yours is good," she snapped back.

"Good," he retorted. "Let us finish up then. We have a long ride ahead of us."

"Will there be someplace for me to freshen up before I meet your people?" She believed in first impressions. She already had enough going against her. She didn't need to add unseemliness. "I must look a mess." She was pushing her hair back and combing it with her fingers.

He sat and watched her. She could never look anything but beautiful. "There is a stream about one hour from the camp. You can take a dip there." Her expression said she was grateful.

They broke camp and rode straight through lunch and dinner. Katrina was getting really sleepy. Her head would start to drop, and she would jerk it back up again. She felt Silver Ghost pull her back against his chest and hold her head there. She wanted to pull away but was too tired to try. Sleep overtook her.

Silver Ghost was constantly amazed at how heavy a sleeper she was. Being a warrior in his tribe meant they were taught to be alert even in their sleep. He would never be able to sleep riding upon a horse, especially through the night.

He had made a good time. They were almost at the stream when the sun was starting to rise. They would be at his camp by the noon meal.

He reined in his horse next to the stream and let him drink. He sat there for a few moments, looking at his wife-to-be. She hadn't woken on her own. She was actually sitting sideways with her head on his shoulder. He had laid her body back a little so that he could study her features. She was so stunning. He knew their children would be good-looking.

Just looking at her was making him uneasy in the saddle. He bent down and brushed her lips lightly. There was no response. He did it again, just a little longer this time. He started to trace her lips with his tongue. Now she was starting to respond. Then she froze. He pulled away to look at her. Confusion was in her features.

He asked her, "Why did you stop?"

Katrina pushed herself out of his arms and got down from the horse.

"Moonglow?" He stopped her in her tracks. "I asked you a question."

She turned on him. Her eyes were shooting daggers at him. "You do not want an answer to that question."

"Yes, I do." He asked her again, "Why did you stop kissing me?"

"Because it was not you I was kissing in my dream. Are you satisfied?" She could see that she had hurt him deeply. She couldn't handle the pain written on his face, so she turned and walked down the stream a ways.

She sat on the side of the bank to think about her dream of Chad. He probably didn't even care. The saying "Out of sight, out of mind" came to mind.

Time was running out for her. If they got to the camp today, she would become Silver Ghost's wife. There would be no turning back after that.

Even if she did manage to get away after they were married, Chad wouldn't want used goods.

She also knew that she would be repeating those vows of marriage. She had promised. She had been raised to keep her word, and the vows were "Till death do you part."

"Damn!" she said aloud. She had to try and escape one more time. Even if Silver Ghost did catch her and rape her, at least she tried one more time. He was going to take her as his wife tonight anyway. What did a few hours difference make? She might as well go down fighting.

Chad was sitting at the kitchen table with Evelyn and Bo. It had been two days since Katrina had disappeared. Bo was telling Chad the same thing he had told his mother the morning she had left.

"It does not sound like she left against her will, Evelyn," Chad tried to point out without causing her any more pain.

When Bo had collected him from Barbara's boarding house, he had told Chad Evelyn was mourning as if Katrina was dead.

"Chad, you do not understand. Katrina left this here." Evelyn pulled out Katrina's diary. "I know she would never leave this behind. She has kept record in it since she was thirteen years old. Her pa gave her this book here, and she has never gone to bed without holdin' it while she is saying her prayers at the foot of her bed. It is like she was with her pa when she holds this book. She feels obligated to him for this gift. She shows her respect to him each night when she puts an entry in this book here. I do not know if she still does it or not, but she used to end with 'I love you, Daddy' at the end of each entry"

Chad was looking at the book that told Katrina's every thought, every wish. "So I am to understand you have not read anything from the last couple of weeks?"

"No! I could never do that, Chad. This book here is very personal," she said, appalled.

Chad snatched the book from her hands. "Well, we need to know what her feelings are, do we not? If she is in love with Silver Ghost and they have gone away to share their love, then we have no right chasing after them, and I will not waste my time." He was holding his breath when he saw "I think I am falling in love with the most wonderful man. I miss you, Pa. I love you, Pa." The lump in his throat almost choked him.

He looked at Evelyn. "As for your question in regard to her father, she still addresses him after each entry." He was afraid to go on. He couldn't read her feelings about Silver Ghost. It was harder than he thought it would be. He handed the book to Evelyn. "She has wrote she thinks she is falling in love with him."

Evelyn looked at the entry then turned to the next page. Chad had gotten up to leave. He should have just told Bo to leave things as they were and not come out to the ranch, but he needed to reassure Evelyn, so he had.

A smile came across Evelyn's face. "Chad?" Her heart was jumping for joy. "I think there is somethin' here you should be lookin' at." Evelyn walked up and put her hand on his shoulder then handed the diary to him.

Chad looked down at the page and saw the broken heart with his name in it next to Katrina's, not Silver Ghost's. Then he read the entry above it. "I do not want to be your little sister, Chad. I want to be your wife."

"Well, I be damned," he whispered.

Evelyn was shocked at his response, so she got angry. "Even if you do not feel for her the way she feels for you, Chad, this is the proof that she is not in love with the Indian and did not leave of her own free will. I want my little girl back, Chad, and you are the one that is going to bring her home to me!" she was yelling at him almost hysterically, on the verge of tears. She didn't know if it was because she was afraid for Katrina or because her heart went out to a man that didn't return the feelings.

Those fears were put to rest shortly after she thought them because Chad picked her up and was twirling her around the kitchen howling. She had begun to think he had gone loco.

Chad set her down and took her by the shoulders. He then looked her straight in the eyes. "Evelyn, you have got it all wrong. Trina means the world to me. I will bring her home but not for anyone but myself." With that, he turned on his heel and marched outside.

Bo had been taking it all in. "That is what I could not tell ya, Ma. Chad was jealous of Silver Ghost. That is why he left in the first place."

Evelyn couldn't be happier for her daughter. She knew Chad would find her, even if it took years. She realized he was going to be on a long trip. She ran to the cupboards to put some staples together for him in a saddlebag. She put lots of coffee in. Knowing Chad, he wouldn't stop to rest until he had found her and would need the caffeine to stay awake.

Bo had walked outside to see where Chad had gone. He found him in the barn.

Chad had gone from being overjoyed to extremely angry. "Chad, you okay?"

"Bo, if I had that Indian in front of me this minute, I think I would be able to shoot him dead on the spot. You know this means Katrina did not want to go with him? You know this means he has probably raped her more than once by now?"

"Chad, let me go with you. If you cannot kill him, I sure as hell can."

"Thanks, Bo, but I have to do this on my own, and I can only pray that Katrina has been able to hold her own, no telling what she has been going through. I just hope I can get to her before he drives her to madness."

Bo gave Chad a big hug. "Godspeed," he told Chad, looking him straight in the eyes. "She loves you, Chad, above all else, remember that. No matter what kind of shape you find her in, bring her home. We will all make her better."

"I will. I will bring her back, and when I do, Bo, know this, I will make her my wife."

"Are you going to be okay with the fact that he might have already made her pregnant?" Bo was watching him closely. "She could be carrying a half-breed, Chad. What are you going to do about that?"

Chad looked down at the ground for a few seconds. When he looked up at Bo, there was so much love in his eyes. "I believe I could work through anything for Katrina. I am not the one that has been abused. It is her, and she needs me to be strong for her. Bo, I have grown to love her completely, and if that means taking on a child that belongs to another man, then so be it."

"Chad, I could not ask for a better man to take care of my sister the rest of her life, but you need to fetch her home first."

With that, Chad mounted Streak and headed out of the barn.

Evelyn was standing on the porch with a sack of provisions. "You are a good woman, Evelyn." He winked at her.

She blushed. "And you are a sweet talker." Then she got serious. Her voice started to crack. "Chad, you bring my little girl home."

As he took the bag of food from Evelyn, he spoke from the heart, "I will not come back without her." He gave Streak a kick, and off they went.

Katrina had just finished putting on the Indian dress that Silver Ghost had insisted she wear. She didn't know how he had gotten a hold of it from the last time she wore it. She could swear she had thrown it away.

She sat on a rock trying to get some of the tangles out of her wet hair. Silver Ghost was up the stream a ways sprawled out on the ground, taking in the sun. She wondered what it would be like to have him make love to her. It probably wouldn't be a bad thing if she loved him, but her heart was always going to belong to Chad.

She continued to finger comb her hair. Silver Ghost hadn't moved for about five minutes. The stream made plenty of noise. She couldn't hear him from here to see if he was snoring. She continued to watch him. His body twitched from sleep. She couldn't believe her luck. He was out.

Fear gripped her whole body. She was shaking so bad. I've got to get a hold of myself. There's got to be a place I can hide. She quickly went back in the water and walked upstream as quietly as she could. The stream would wash away her tracks. She walked past him, holding her breath. She stepped on as many stones as she could to leave less of a trail. It was slow going, and she almost fell in once. The splash would have woken him in a heartbeat.

When he was completely out of sight from her, she waded across the stream to the other side. On the bank, there was a boulder, so she climbed on it instead of leaving tracks on the ground. She wasn't sure where to go. She just kept hopping from one rock to the next. She wanted to make it as hard as possible for him to pick up her trail.

She was huffing and puffing from the exertion of climbing and hopping, but she knew she had to keep going. Silver Ghost was a tracker by nature, and she couldn't let him find her.

She had been gone for about a half hour now. Her feet hadn't touched the ground once. Surely that was good enough to hit the ground and start running. That's exactly what she did. She ran until her lungs burned and she couldn't run anymore. She was bending over, trying to catch her breath when she realized her head was making a pounding noise. No! That wasn't her head because it was getting louder. It was horse hooves pounding on the ground at a fast pace, coming her way.

"No!" she cried. "How could he have found me so easily?" She stood feeling defeated, and then she saw the rider. It wasn't Silver Ghost. No, it was an Indian but not Silver Ghost. Katrina took off running as fast as she could, but with one swoop, she was lifted off the ground and slammed down on the horse in front of her abductor.

She tried to twist and turn to get away, but his arms were like shackles around her, and she was so exhausted.

They rode for about an hour. Her ribs were killing her. She couldn't believe her luck. What had she ever done to deserve the way her life was going? All she ever wanted was to grow old on her ranch, maybe someday have a family of her own, but even that thought hadn't been one until recently.

When they finally stopped, she noticed she was in a camp where Indian children were running around with dogs. Women were tending to chores, but all had stopped to look at her.

Her abductor got off the horse, taking her with him. He pulled her into a tepee. "Sit," he ordered.

Katrina sat and watched his back as he walked out.

She lay down. The skins she lay on were so soft. She covered her face with both arms over her head. She wasn't going to cry. She just wasn't.

Katrina heard the flap of the tepee open, so she sat up quickly and saw a pretty woman, who looked to be in her early forties, enter. Her hair was done in a braid that Katrina had never seen before. She was slender and graceful as she moved about the tepee.

The woman spoke English, "Did my son hurt you, child?"

Katrina sat before her looking a mess. Her hair was all tangled. She didn't have a chance to answer before the woman asked another question. "You wear clothes of my people. How is this?" Her voice wasn't harsh, just curious.

Katrina asked as the light went on in her head, "Is there a Silver Ghost who lives among you?"

The woman's head snapped up. "How is it you know my son?" The question was so sharp Katrina shied away from the harshness. The woman noticed this. "I am sorry if I frightened you." She approached Katrina. "My son is Silver Ghost. He has been gone for too long this time. I almost gave him up for dead. Again, how is it you know my son?"

It was making sense to Katrina now. "I was with him until just this morning. I tried to run away but was taken by the boy who brought me here." There was disappointment in her voice.

The happiness of Silver Ghost still being alive was apparent in the woman's eyes. She spoke, "That was my youngest son, Bear Claw. My name is Morning Dew. What do your people call you?"

"Your son calls me Moonglow." Morning Dew's face lit up with this news.

"My son has named you well. Why were you trying to run away from him? Has he hurt you?"

"No!" Katrina answered quickly, "He has not hurt me physically. He has just taken me to be his wife, and I do not want to be his wife."

Morning Dew was a little surprised. Any woman that Silver Ghost chose from the camp would be honored to be his. "Why is this?" she asked Katrina curiously.

"I love someone else, but Silver Ghost does not seem to care. He told me his grandfather would marry us when we reached camp, and then he would take me as his."

Morning Dew was a little confused. "Moonglow, do you mind if I call you that, or would you rather me call you by your given name?"

"My name is Katrina," she answered quickly.

"Okay, then, Katrina. What Silver Ghost failed to explain to you is there are no forced weddings with our people. If you were to marry my son, which would be a great honor for you, it would have to be of your own free will."

"What?" Katrina jumped up. She was filled all of a sudden with all the fight she used to have. "How dare he. He led me to believe I had no choice at all. Once the marriage was consummated, he knew I would stay with him. I do have my honor." Katrina stomped her foot. She was so furious that she almost scared Morning Dew.

Morning Dew approached her. "Calm down, child. We will get this straightened out as soon as Bear Claw returns with Silver Ghost." No sooner did she say it when they heard the camp break out in elation of Silver Ghost's return.

Morning Dew took Katrina's hand to lead her outside. Katrina was shaking from head to toe. She was afraid of what Silver Ghost was going to do to her.

Morning Dew ran to him. "My son, I am so glad you have come home to us," she spoke to him in their own tongue.

He also spoke to her in his native tongue. The whole time, he had eye contact with Katrina. "I am also glad to be home although this is not exactly how I had planned it. I see my princess arrived safely."

All eyes turned to Katrina. She felt panicked.

Morning Dew answered him, "Yes, she has, but she has also told me a few things that I am not happy to hear, my son."

Silver Ghost abruptly turned his attention back to his mother. "Like what? I have not laid a hand on her. I have been waiting for our vows." He was defensive.

"That is what I want to talk to you about, the marriage. She says she does not consent to marrying you. Is this true?"

He kissed her lightly on the cheek. "Leave things to me, Morning Dew. She will consent. In the meantime, I have a bone to pick with her, and I do not want to be disturbed. Do I make myself clear?" She saw something she hadn't seen in her son before. She wasn't sure if it was love or not, but she could see determination in his eyes.

"No, my son, you will not be disturbed." She moved aside and let him pass.

Silver Ghost walked toward Katrina. She started to back away but stumbled over the rope for the tepee. Silver Ghost caught her just in time. He lifted her in his arms to carry her into the tepee. All the camp cheered. Katrina ducked her head into his shoulder.

Once they were inside, she scolded him, "Let go of me." She was squirming to get out of his arms.

He put her down. "What are you so angry about? I am the one that should be angry, but instead, I am elated because you have brought upon yourself what I have wanted all along. I expect you to not fight me. You knew the consequences."

"Well, you expect too much, Silver Ghost. I will never submit to you willingly," she spat at him.

"We will just see about that." He grabbed her with one arm and wrapped the other around her waist. He got a death grip in her hair and tilted her head back. He kissed her with such urgency she thought she would have bruises all over her mouth. His kiss was hot and searing, as if he were trying to brand her. He pulled away, breathing hard.

"You are an animal, Silver Ghost." He covered her mouth again, and this time the kiss was softer, teasing her until she started to respond to him.

She didn't want this to happen. This was not Chad. She needed Chad. She was starting to feel warm all over. She couldn't let this happen. She had to get away. She couldn't think. She had learned something. What was it? No, no. "*No!*" she finally was able to scream. She pushed with all her might. "Just stop. I have something to tell you."

"It can wait until after," he boasted sheepishly.

"No!" she barked. "There will be no after, and there will be no wedding vows. You lied to me. I do not have to suffer your consequences. I ran because I did not know I would have a choice when we got here. According to your mother, I do have a choice, and I do not have to marry you or suffer any consequences." She was so out of breath.

"First off, my little princess. I assure you you would not suffer by my touch. You were submitting to me just then." He saw the shock of the truth in her face and laughed. "And second, you would learn there would be nothing but the desire of looking forward to our bedding," he mocked.

"Never!" she cried. "I will never lie with you willingly."

"I promise you, Moonglow, I will never rape you. When we do bed together, I will have your consent. You will even beg me to help you find release." He grabbed her and gave her a hungry kiss. When she started to respond, he released her roughly, shoving her away, and stormed out of the tepee.

She stood there fuming. What did he mean by begging for release? He was right about her starting to respond to him. His touch wasn't repulsive anymore. She had to keep her head straight.

She lay on the bedding and thought of what she needed to do next. She couldn't let him touch her. She seemed to lose the ability to think straight when he touched her anymore. She was exhausted from all the emotional turmoil. That is what it was. She closed her eyes. She needed to make a plan. She started to fall asleep and woke with a start, berating herself, "Do not dare fall asleep, Katrina. You have to think." Her eyes drifted shut again, and sleep overtook her before she could come up with that plan.

Katrina didn't know how long she had slept before she felt a presence. She opened her eyes to see Morning Dew shuffling about. Katrina sat up and stretched.

"I am glad to see you are awake. We have very little time."

"Little time for what?"

"The feast of course. My son has returned, and since he is the appointed chief, we will celebrate his return with a feast," she said with pride in her voice.

"I do not feel much like celebrating, especially when Silver Ghost is the guest of honor. I hope you will excuse me."

"Nonsense, Katrina. It would be very disrespectable for a guest to miss out on the chief's return feast. I will not hear of it. Now here." Morning Dew held out a beautiful leather dress. The neckline, hem, and waist had tiny beads sewn into it. It had been dyed sky blue. "This ought to fit you nicely." Morning Dew was glowing from the excitement. She had had a long talk with Silver Ghost this afternoon, and he had reassured her that Katrina was not in any danger by him, that he loved her and wanted more than anything to make her happy. Morning Dew believed her son, and she wanted to see this beautiful young woman fall in love with her son. They would make a handsome couple.

Katrina reluctantly took the dress. It had to be better than what she was already wearing. "I will leave you to change, then I will return and do your hair."

Morning Dew exited the tepee, and Katrina rushed to put the dress on. She had just pulled it over her head when Silver Ghost walked in. "Oh," she covered herself quickly. She was blushing. "You could have at least knocked."

He laughed. "And what would you have me knock on?" He was pleased to see she had put on the dress he had picked out for her. She didn't need to know it was his choice though. The dress fit her in all the right places. She was very full in her breast, and her tiny waist only made her look even larger. He would have a hard time keeping his eyes off her tonight. As a matter of fact, the whole tribe would be envious of him tonight.

"Well, you could at least signal somehow so this will not happen again." Her voice was shaking. The way he was looking at her made her very uncomfortable.

"What would you have me do, Moonglow?" He was teasing her now, all the while not taking his hungry eyes off her.

"I do not know. Whistle or something?" she roared.

"Okay, fine. How is this?" He demonstrated a wolf-call whistle, which caused Katrina to blush.

"Would you get out of here? I need to get ready for the celebration in your honor," she sounded like a jealous, spoiled child.

"You act like you have something better to do." He was laughing as he left her.

CHAPTER EIGHT

An hour later, Katrina was sitting next to Morning Dew. She looked absolutely radiant even with her pouty lip. Morning Dew had put her hair in a double herringbone braid. Her hair was so long it lay on the ground on both sides of her.

The dress was very low-cut. Her cleavage is what drew everyone's attention. Silver Ghost wasn't too sure he liked sharing that much of her with everyone.

She sat on her knees, anticipating what was to come. She wasn't sure of what to expect.

The drums started pounding, and a beautiful Indian girl, Katrina would have to guess to be about seventeen, came out dancing. At first, she seemed to dance for everyone, then her attention turned strictly to Silver Ghost. Katrina watched him as his expression grew lustful. Katrina was boiling inside. What was he doing? He was supposed to be marrying her, not gawking over another woman.

She chided herself. She wasn't jealous. No! It was that he was making her look like a fool. She could feel people staring at her to see what she was going to do.

Silver Ghost was watching her out of the corner of his eye. She seemed uneasy with him dancing with another woman. Hopefully she was jealous. He decided to take things to the limit. Little Dove was begging for his company, so why not give it?

Katrina watched in disbelief as Silver Ghost and the girl danced in a very seductive manner. It looked like they were mating with their clothes on. Katrina had had enough. She wasn't going to sit here and watch him make a fool out of her.

She got up and headed for her tepee. She gasped in alarm when a warm hand grabbed her's.

"Do not be frightened, child. I wish you no harm." This Indian looked ancient to say the least, but his eyes spoke the truth. "Come with me." He pulled her along as he walked around the outside of the camp.

"Where are you taking me?" Katrina was growing a little uneasy because of the distance they had gone. She stopped and pulled her hand free from his then repeated her question. "Where are we going?"

"Only to a quiet spot to talk. I will not harm you in any way. I promise." He started to walk again, so she followed.

She asked from behind him, "Who are you anyway?"

They came to a clearing, and he sat, patting the tree trunk next to him. "Here, sit down. I am Sly Fox. I am Silver Ghost's grandfather." He squared his shoulders with pride.

"Why are you not at the celebration?" Katrina wasn't sure if she believed him to be Silver Ghost's grandfather.

"It is not time yet. As the elder, I make a grand entry just before the meal to give thanks to our maker."

Chad rode from morning's first dawn to evening's sundown. He only stopped because he couldn't see the tracks anymore. Their tracks weren't as hard to keep to this time. He was exhausted. He didn't know how much longer it would take. So far, it had been six days. Each and every night, he would wonder if Katrina was safe. Then he would try not to think of what could be happening to her every night. He felt almost hopeless at times, sick to his stomach. He had to find her.

After reading her diary, he knew she loved him and was determined to take care of her the rest of her life. He wasn't sure what he was going to do to Silver Ghost when he found them. At this stage, he didn't think it was going to be a pretty sight.

Chad was just starting his campfire when he heard the noise. He stood up and listened hard. It was drums, way off in the distance.

He ran over to Streak, and they took off. He was elated. If he was close enough to hear the drums, he could protect her as of this night. "Finally!" he rejoiced.

Sly Fox was addressing Katrina, "My grandson is quite taken with you, but I sense the feelings are not returned."

Katrina sat timidly. "I wish I could say you were wrong, but you are not."

"Do you know why?" His concern was genuine.

"I do." She paused and took a deep breath then continued. "My heart belongs to another. Your grandson seems to think he can change that."

Sly Fox sat quietly for a few moments then asked, "Do you think he can change your feelings?"

"I truly do not know. I do not want to hurt him. He really, in all honesty, has not been bad to me. It is just that I was given no choice. He made all the decisions for me. I did not even get to say goodbye to my family. I did not even get to bring my diary." Her voice was so sad.

"Silver Ghost has always been one to act out his own personal life without much advice from this old man, but I will have words with him. He has been used to getting his way far too long."

"Thank you" was her simple response. She started to say more, but the drums had stopped, and you could hear a lot of commotion going on in the camp. They both got up at the same time and started running.

Katrina was amazed at the stamina the old man had. She could hardly keep up with him.

When they ran into the clearing for the camp, they could see a fight had broken out. Katrina assumed it was over the girl that had been dancing, but as she moved closer, she could see it wasn't an Indian against an Indian. It was Silver Ghost and Chad!

"Chad!" she screamed. She saw the knife in Silver Ghost's hand. The two of them were rolling all over the place. Silver Ghost had a cut on his lip.

The realization that Chad was here for her finally hit her. She grabbed Sly Fox and yelled into his ear. "He is the man that holds my heart."

Sly Fox nodded at several warriors, who stepped forward and pulled Chad and Silver Ghost apart.

Katrina ran into Chad's arms. He held her tightly. She could feel his chest rising and falling from his labored breathing. She clung to him as a lifeline.

Katrina looked up at Chad. She could see the hatred he was directing at Silver Ghost. Without breaking eye contact with Silver Ghost, Chad gritted his teeth and asked Katrina, "Did he hurt you, Trina?"

"No," her voice trembled.

"Do not lie to me, Trina. I will not stand for it." Chad's tone was very unforgiving.

Katrina pulled away from him at this point. "Chad, I am not lying. He did not hurt me."

Chad felt the emptiness as soon as she pulled away. He was so glad to have her in his arms. He wanted her back. His feelings were so jumbled. All the way here, he kept telling himself that it wouldn't matter if Silver Ghost had taken her virginity. He had come to terms that there was no way they could have traveled together as long as they had and Silver Ghost not have taken advantage of her. She was such an innocent in such matters.

Maybe she didn't understand the question, so he rephrased it. "Did he rape you, Trina?"

She turned white. "No!"

He still wasn't satisfied. "Did you submit to him?" All of a sudden, it really mattered.

The whole time, Silver Ghost struggled to get free of his own men. They weren't about to let him go.

Sly Fox could see both men were still heated up, and he needed to intervene. Katrina never had the opportunity to answer Chad's last question before Sly Fox addressed Silver Ghost.

"It seems that she seeks another for comfort."

Silver Ghost was still struggling to fill his lungs with air. "She will be my wife, and no one can stop me."

Chad pulled Katrina back into his embrace. "I say differently." He spat the words at Silver Ghost.

Sly Fox spoke to Chad. "It is our custom when two warriors want the same woman. They fight to prove who is the worthier one for her." Katrina gasped at his words.

Morning Dew hated to go against her own son, but she knew the truth and wanted it to be known for Katrina's sake. Her son, no matter what he thought, could not force someone to love him. "It is also our custom that both people consent to vows, Sly Fox. That is not the case."

Silver Ghost could not believe his own mother was turning against him.

Sly Fox looked at Katrina. "Is this so? Do you wish to marry this man who holds you?"

Katrina was scared. She didn't think Chad wanted to hear her wishes. She was too proud to admit such a thing. He wasn't here because he loved her after all. He was here out of loyalty to her family.

"I know I do not wish to marry your grandson. He took me against my will."

Chad was glad to hear she didn't want to marry Silver Ghost, but what did she mean about him taking her against her will? So she had been raped? And why didn't she say Chad was the one she wanted to marry?

"I see," Sly Fox consented.

"Well, I do not." Silver Ghost was fuming. He knew that Katrina loved Chad, but he wasn't sure it was the other way around. "If she is not to marry me, she will marry him . . . tonight."

"No!" Katrina cried out. She didn't want Chad forced into marrying her. She felt him tense up and knew he didn't like the idea of marrying her.

Chad couldn't believe her protest. If he hadn't read her diary, he would think she didn't want to marry him. What was her problem?

"The way I see it, Moonglow, you do not have a choice," Silver Ghost was mocking her. "It is either him or me tonight."

"She will marry me," Chad spoke up. "Let us get this over with."

Katrina felt defeated. Chad was just being loyal to her family. She would tell him tonight that he could have the marriage annulled as soon as they got home.

Sly Fox stepped forward. "Let us get the vows underway."

Katrina looked up at Chad. She couldn't tell what he was thinking. He looked angry.

He was angry. Did she really not want to marry him? Did she fall out of love with him? Chad grabbed her hand and held it tightly.

The ceremony was over before Katrina knew it. There was no feeling in the words. She felt cold all over. Marrying Chad was the one thing in the world she did want to do because she loved him, but for him to be forced had ruined any chance they would ever have. Chad would never forgive her for this mess.

Several of the warriors erected a shelter for their honeymoon quarters.

Chad would rather have gotten back on his horse and headed out, but he didn't want to insult anyone.

"Suddenly I am very tired," Katrina confessed.

"Then we will turn in," Chad spoke softly to her, and then he turned to the group that had gathered around them. "Good night, all." Everyone cheered. It seemed to be the right thing to say.

Silver Ghost looked on with disgust. He hoped the marriage turned out sour. Chad didn't look pleased with the whole situation. This pleased Silver Ghost immensely.

Katrina went to the bedding and sat rigidly. Chad wasn't sure of what to say to her to ease her fears. He was a little nervous himself. Okay, maybe a lot.

Katrina finally broke the silence. "Chad, you do not really consider this a real marriage, do you? After all, he was not a preacher or anyone appointed by the church to marry people."

The muscle worked in Chad's jaw. When he finally spoke, the exhaustion from the last week came forth. "Trina, it was a marriage spoken in front of God. It does not matter if a preacher did it or not. The vows were said." Now that she was his, he wasn't going to let her go. If she wanted to repeat vows in front of her family and friends at a later date, that was fine with him, but as far as he was concerned, she was his wife now.

Katrina read disgust in his voice. She felt it was toward the fact that he was forced to marry her. She snapped at him, "Fine, then when we get home, we will have it annulled."

"Is that what you really want?" His voice was hoarse.

"Yes," she barely whispered. She didn't really, but she knew Chad didn't love her, and she would only marry for love.

"Fine" was his final word. He crawled onto the bedding and faced the wall, with his back to her. He didn't bother removing any of his clothes and neither did she.

It was a long while before she heard his even breathing. Her tears started to come openly now. She couldn't hold them back anymore. As she lay there, Chad rolled over and put his arm around her waist. He pulled her close to him but continued to sleep the whole time. It made her cry harder. She snuggled into him and finally fell asleep.

When Chad woke the next morning, Katrina was sleeping with her head in the crook of his arm. He looked at her and could see her eyes and nose were swollen. Had she been crying? The many times they had slept out on the range, he didn't remember her waking up puffy.

Chad kissed her eyes softly. She didn't stir. He kissed her cheek then her mouth. When she responded to him, he drew back to look at her. Her eyes were still closed. Chad smiled and kissed her again. Katrina opened for him, and he was pleasantly surprised. Chad cherished the kiss.

Katrina was having the most wonderful dream. Chad was kissing her with all the love she felt for him. When she opened her eyes, she realized it hadn't been a dream.

Chad smiled down on her. "Good morning."

Katrina jumped out of the bed. "What were you thinking?" She didn't want Chad to play games with her. This was her heart that was going to break again after all.

"When I woke, you were snuggled up so sweetly next to me I could not resist."

"Well, resist in the future. I am not one of those barmaids you like to play with." She grabbed her belongings. "I want to go home," she finished as she huffed out of the tepee.

Chad sat there for a second. Did she find his kisses that repulsive? She didn't act like it when she first responded to him. Why was she so angry with him? He thought she would like the idea of being married to him. Maybe he misunderstood her diary. He didn't think so. He got his belongings together and went outside.

Katrina was talking to Sly Fox. He was offering her a horse to take as a gift for all her trouble. She accepted it gladly so she wouldn't have to ride with Chad on the way home.

She walked over to Silver Ghost. Chad watched, his stomach in knots. He didn't like the way Silver Ghost was looking at her.

"I should have taken you the first time I wanted to. I should have made you my wife before we ever got here, then you would still be mine." Silver Ghost grabbed her and planted a long breathtaking kiss on her. "It is not over," he stated matter-of-factly, and then he pushed her away.

Chad had started toward them when Silver Ghost had grabbed her, but Sly Fox put his hand on Chad's shoulder. "She is yours now," he simply said.

Katrina went to slap Silver Ghost but missed. Just the idea that she wanted to hit him gave Chad a little satisfaction. He wanted to do more, like rearrange his face.

"It is over, Silver Ghost. I am a married woman now, and there is nothing you can do about it." She felt a little justified until his expression turned serious.

His words sent a chill down her spine. "You will be mine again one day, Moonglow. Mark my words."

Chad had had enough. This conversation was over as far as he was concerned. Silver Ghost was messing with Katrina's head, and he wouldn't have it.

Katrina had started to walk away from Silver Ghost. She didn't want to listen to this nonsense. Chad walked up and took her by the shoulders for them to both face Silver Ghost.

Chad's nostrils were flaring. "Now you mark my words." Chad gritted his teeth. "She is *my* wife, and I take that responsibility very seriously. You stay away from her. Do I make myself clear?"

Silver Ghost gave Chad a deadly stare.

Chad turned to the horses and helped Katrina mount. He then mounted Streak and looked at Silver Ghost again. "Do not make me have to kill you, Silver Ghost. At this point, I would not think twice." Chad kicked his horse, and they were headed home.

Katrina could only hope that it was the last she saw of Silver Ghost. But something in her gut told her it wasn't.

They had ridden for about an hour in silence. Chad could tell Katrina was disturbed by Silver Ghost's words. He needed to help her feel secure.

"Trina?" She jumped because it had been so quiet. She had been in such deep thought.

"What?"

"I think I have something that will help you feel a little safer. Let's water the horses here, and I will get it."

They were at the stream where she had made her big escape.

She dismounted. She would be so glad to be home. This last two months had been so unreal. She just wanted things to be normal again.

Chad approached her with her handgun. He had had it in his saddlebag. "Here, keep this close. That should help you feel safer."

"And what do you think I am going to do with it? Kill Silver Ghost? I do not think I could do that, Chad. It is one thing to kill an animal that is attacking you, but a human being is another story."

"Katrina, if your life were in danger, I do not think it would matter what was attacking you. If Silver Ghost tries to make good on his word, it might be your only defense. Just keep it close. That is all I am asking of you."

"Chad, do you really think he is going to give me any more trouble?"

He didn't want to scare her, but he truly didn't believe they had seen the last of Silver Ghost.

"I really do not know, Trina. Just be prepared. Okay?" He had walked up to her and put his hands on her shoulders. She was looking down. "Look at me." She looked up. "I promise you I will protect you with my life." He was looking her directly in the eyes. "Do you trust me?" She nodded. "Good. Now let's get you home. Your poor ma has got to be going out of her mind again."

Just the mention of her mom made her want to rush. "Can we ride hard, Chad?"

"We will take it as best we can without putting either of us in danger. I will let you decide when you need to rest. Okay?"

"Okay." She smiled for the first time in days. Chad made her feel safe.

The only time they stopped in forty-eight hours was to eat and stretch. Katrina was pushing hard. He didn't know if it was the need to get home and get her annulment or that she just didn't want to sleep next to him. Without stopping, they were more than halfway home already.

Chad noticed the clouds coming their way. It looked like they were in for a lot of rain. He wasn't too happy about the situation. They would have no shelter.

When it started to rain, Chad grabbed his slicker out of his saddlebag. "You better ride with me for a while, Trina. We can share the slicker to stay drier."

Katrina reined in next to Chad. He lifted her from her horse and put her in front of him. The slicker would just barely go around the two of them. She buttoned it as he continued to ride. She had to admit it was cozy and warmer. She hadn't realized how cold it had gotten. She had been in a state of numbness since they had started out.

She couldn't quit thinking about Silver Ghost's last words.

"You have been awful quiet. Are you okay?" His mouth was right next to her ear, and his warm breath gave her goose bumps.

"I am," she replied. She could feel his heartbeat on her back. That was how close they were.

"That's my girl," he praised her.

If only that was true. She wished to be his girl. She wished things were different. Maybe if he hadn't been forced to marry her, she could have helped him to grow fond of her. Being forced to marry had to have been a big turnoff for him; after all, he didn't even try to consummate their marriage.

What a funny thought, she chided herself. With Silver Ghost, she had been dreading even the thought. With Chad, she was disappointed that he wasn't interested. What a mess!

Chad was glad to have her wrapped in his arms. Even if he had to find the excuse of the rain, he felt good.

So many times, he had thanked the Lord for her safety. He also thanked the Lord for the luck of her being his wife. She thought they would get it annulled when they got home, but if he had anything to say about it, she would stay his wife. He hoped that in this week that they traveled home, he could persuade her to stay married. He never was one for getting his feelings out right, and he was afraid of mucking it up.

They rode in silence for hours. The silence was driving her nuts. "Chad, I am getting hungry. Do you think we could stop soon?"

"Sure." His breath was warm and made her shiver.

"Are you cold?" Chad pulled her closer to him. He could feel the temperature dropping. "Can you hold out for about a half hour? We will stop and set up camp then. It is going to be a miserable night, I am sorry to say."

"We will make due," she assured him.

A few minutes later, they came across a broken-down buckboard. "Look, Trina, we can rig that up for shelter tonight."

"Of all the luck," she approved.

They worked together to turn the buckboard up on its side to rest against two trees. Chad built a fire at the end so it wouldn't fill up with smoke. Katrina took the bedroll out and laid it out in the driest area she could find. It was getting colder by the second. "Do you think it is going to snow, Chad?"

"I do not know. We are high enough that it could. Let's just hope not." It had already occurred to him that it might. They could freeze to death if it did.

They sat huddled eating a pheasant. "This is nice," Katrina stated.

"Yes, it is," he agreed.

Chad had been keeping his eye on her ever since they stopped. The only time he didn't seem to be staring a hole through her was when she pardoned herself for some privacy.

She looked up now, and their eyes met. She wished she knew what he was thinking. "Yes, well," she broke the spell, "I guess I will turn in."

"I will join you in a few minutes." He put the slicker on and left the shelter.

Katrina mumbled, "You were right when you said it was going to be a miserable night."

Chad walked out in the rain. He wanted to give her some privacy and do some cooling off himself. How he was going to sleep next to her all night and keep his hands to himself was beyond him.

He sat out under a tree a couple yards from her. She was lying down but not asleep. She was too restless to be asleep. It had been about thirty minutes, and he was getting chilled to the bone. He looked up and only saw black. There was no star in the sky. It was going to be a cold one tonight.

They would need each other's body heat to keep warm, and that's what worried him. His body would react to her too fast, and if she realized what was on his mind, she would be appalled.

Katrina tried to sleep, but sleep wouldn't come. Chad had been gone a long time. She was starting to get worried. She tossed and turned. She was starting to get cold. Would Chad at least cuddle her to keep her warm? she wondered.

The rain hadn't let up at all. They could even get snow if the temperature kept dropping. She sat up. She was really starting to worry about him.

Chad saw her sitting up. It was doing him no good sitting out in the cold. He was hoping she would fall asleep, but it was no use. He ran back to their shelter.

"I was starting to worry about you," she confessed quietly.

"No reason to worry. I did not go far." He smiled at her wearily. "Do you have room for me in there?"

"As a matter of fact, I have got a spot with your name on it right here." She patted next to her.

Chad shrugged out of the slicker and crawled over to where she had patted. After she lay back down, he pulled the slicker over their blanket.

They were lying on their sides facing each other. They each used their own arm as a pillow. "Are you okay?" he asked, not knowing what else to say.

"Yes, you?"

"Yes." After a moment, he stated, "It is going to get pretty cold tonight."

"I kind of guessed that myself. We only have this one blanket and the slicker. I am afraid we might freeze." She shivered.

"I will not let that happen."

"Oh? And how do you plan on preventing it?" She smiled at him.

"I think we might have to get naked." He knew he would shock her with his words.

"What?" She choked. She wasn't expecting that answer.

Chad chuckled at her expression. It was the truth though. The best body heat was two bodies together without clothing as a barrier. If the truth were known, he would like nothing better than to cuddle naked next to his wife. He really was growing fond of the thought.

"Do not worry, Trina. I do not think it will get that cold, but you do know what I say is true."

"I do know, Chad," she said shyly.

"Here, turn around, and let me cuddle your back. The gap between us is too much."

He helped her turn over without the blanket and slicker falling off. He pulled her snug up against him. "Is that better?" He was warmer already. He had put extra wood inside so he could keep stoking the fire through the night. They would be fine.

Katrina felt cherished. She felt safe, and she felt protected. She knew Chad would take good care of her. If all went well, they would be home in two days. They could even ride all the rest of the way. They had made it two days straight already. But then again, another night in Chad's arms would be worth another day. Then sadness came over her. She wanted this forever, and she didn't know how to let Chad know. Somehow she would have to get him to see that she could make him a good wife. But how? She definitely didn't have any experience in this area.

"Go to sleep, my little Trina." He knew her mind was working too hard on something. She was probably worried he was going to take advantage of her. He cared for her too much to ever do that. "I promise you are safe with me."

"I know, Chad. Thank you." She was quiet for a moment. She loved it when he called her his little Trina. "Thank you for coming after me again, Chad. I should have thanked you earlier."

"I would not have sent anyone else, Trina." She was his, and he intended to make that claim when they got home and a real preacher could marry them. She would see that he could be a good husband to her. Somehow he would make her see.

Chad could tell when she had finally let sleep take her. He pulled her even closer. It was going to get really cold, but he intended to keep her warm.

When Chad and Katrina woke the next morning, there was about three inches of snow on the ground. Neither of them wanted to come out from under their little cocoon.

Chad leaned up on one elbow. "We might need to ride together, Trina. We can keep the blanket and slicker on us for warmth that way."

"Okay," she answered with a hidden smile. She would like nothing better than to sit next to him for the next couple of days.

"You ready? We can alternate on the horses so that we can go farther."

"Okay." She had decided last night to drag it out if she could, but riding next to him was just as good.

They heard their horses whinnying. Both of them got up to see Silver Ghost scaring them off.

Silver Ghost made an awful shrill that echoed in the hills.

Katrina yelled at him, "What are you doing? Have you lost your mind?"

Silver Ghost only laughed.

Chad was afraid she wasn't too far off the mark. "What do you want, Silver Ghost?" Chad asked, as if he didn't already know.

"I want what is mine." He hopped off his horse.

"And what do you think is yours here, Silver Ghost, *my* wife?"

Silver Ghost took that as a challenge, which Chad was hoping for, and charged Chad. Katrina screamed. This was not happening. What was she going to do? Silver Ghost seemed to have an advantage over Chad. He was angrier. At least at first it seemed that way, but Katrina saw something in Chad's eyes—determination. Then it was gone. Silver Ghost had picked up a good-sized rock as they had been rolling on the ground and crushed it on Chad's head.

Chad was out cold. Katrina ran to him but didn't make it. Silver Ghost grabbed her. "He is dead, Moonglow, and now I will have you. You belong to me."

At first, she wasn't hearing him. She couldn't take her eyes off Chad as Silver Ghost was pulling her along. Then what he was saying started registering. "No!" she yelled at him as she pulled herself out of his grasp. "You are wrong, Silver Ghost. I do not belong to you. I belong to Chad."

Silver Ghost was so fast she didn't even have time to blink. He had her on the bedding that she and Chad had shared. He was going to rape her. The look in his eyes said it all. Katrina was screaming at him to get off. She was pulling his hair, scratching at his face, and biting his arms. Nothing was getting to him.

Chad could hear her screaming. He tried to get up, but he passed out again.

Silver Ghost had pulled her dress up around her waist. He was straddling her so she couldn't move away. Katrina was trying to find her gun that Chad had given her. She had put it under the blanket. She knew it had to be there. Silver Ghost was sliding his chaps down his hips with one hand, and he held her captive with the other. She was screaming at him to stop. He wasn't listening. He had a look in his eyes she hadn't seen. It was like he was a different person. Where was that damn gun?

"Silver Ghost, I said *stop*! Get off me. Don't do this."

Chad could feel the pistol in his hand. Katrina's screaming was desperate. He couldn't even lift his head, but he lifted the gun and shot anyway, then there was silence.

Silver Ghost was just positioning himself to enter her; she could feel him between her legs. She was going to throw up when she heard gunfire.

Everything seemed to stop. The weight of Silver Ghost falling on top of her took her breath away. He was so heavy.

She couldn't move. He was too big. Then she felt the warmth of his blood running down her cheek. She couldn't stand it. She pushed with all her might, and the adrenaline alone helped her to shove him off.

CHAPTER NINE

Katrina looked around and found Chad had crawled closer to her. He was lying very still with the smoking gun in his hand. It was the very same gun she had been looking for. She ran to him. He was facedown in the snow.

"Chad," she sobbed. His head was bleeding terribly, so she put pressure on his head to get the blood to stop flowing. When she felt the bleeding had slowed enough, she grabbed one of his shirts and put snow in it then tied it around his head. She hoped it would help to keep the swelling down.

She needed to make Chad comfortable. He was shivering from the cold or possibly shock. Which of the two, she wasn't sure. Katrina looked up and saw Silver Ghost's dead body and shivered. "Chad, I need to leave you for a moment." When he grabbed her wrist, she reassured him, "I will not be long. I promise."

Katrina placed his head on the ground and hurried over to the body of Silver Ghost. Chad had shot him in the side of the head. He was almost unrecognizable. Katrina wanted to throw up, but she knew Chad needed her. She used every bit of her inner strength and determination to move Silver Ghost's body. She grabbed his body from under his arms and pulled with all her might to get him out from under the shelter. It wasn't easy; he was a big man. Then in the same manner, she tried to pull Chad into the shelter, but he was much heavier. "Chad, can you use your legs and push with me? I need to get you under the shelter." It was slow going, but she finally made him comfortable on the bed. Once she was done with the moving of both of them, she collapsed from sheer exhaustion.

After she caught her breath, she restarted the fire and lay next to Chad to help him get warm. Chad hadn't quit shaking.

"Please, Chad, you have to fight. Please do not leave me out here alone. I need you," she pleaded. She felt helpless. She couldn't think of anything more she could do for him.

She just lay there, holding him while he shook, rubbing his arms to make a friction, and hoping it was helping.

The day wore on. She had gotten up a couple of times to give him fluids. He wasn't responding to her. She kept talking to him, mostly nonsense about her childhood on the ranch before she had met him, but she felt if she could keep his senses alert by trying to concentrate on a voice, his mind wouldn't shut down.

That evening, Chad had a fitful night. He tossed and turned, moaning in pain. At least he kept reassuring her that he was still alive.

The following morning, he rested peacefully. Katrina kept watching him to make sure his chest was rising and falling. She had run out of things to talk about, so she decided to sing songs to keep his mind stimulated.

She had killed a rabbit and boiled it so she could spoon-feed him broth. He needed fluids and nourishment to keep his strength up.

Katrina had fallen asleep just from exhaustion. The vision of Silver Ghost standing over her kept haunting her. She didn't sleep very long.

She got up and decided she needed to bury Silver Ghost's body. Although she didn't feel he deserved a burial, she didn't want his dead body attracting hungry animals.

The digging was good for her body and soul. It took her almost two days to dig a hole big enough. She would alternate between taking care of Chad and digging.

Silver Ghost's body making a thump into the hole when she pushed it in was closure for her. She felt like she would be able to put this whole ordeal behind her; after all, he didn't succeed in raping her. She was still whole for Chad, and she definitely was going to be Chad's. She still wasn't sure how, but she knew it for a fact.

Katrina was just finishing covering up Silver Ghost with the dirt when she heard Chad call out. She dropped everything and ran to him.

He was sitting up, holding his head. His eyes were still closed, so she wasn't sure he was even awake. Katrina sat next to him and put her hand on his leg. "Chad?" she spoke softly. She couldn't imagine how bad his head must hurt.

He opened one eye and looked at her. What a pathetic sight he made. Both of his eyes were swollen. He still had some dried blood on the side of his head, and he still wore the shirt she had tied onto his head with snow in it.

"How do you feel?" Katrina choked on her words. She was so happy he was going to be okay.

Chad sat there for a while. He was trying to remember what had happened. He felt like he'd been run over by a stagecoach being pulled by a twenty-horse team. He knew his head was killing him right now and needed to lie back down. Katrina helped him. As he lay there, some of his memory started coming back. He remembered hearing Katrina screaming. He remembered the Indian over her body. "Oh god," he moaned.

"What is it? What can I do, Chad?" She wanted to make it all better but felt powerless.

He spoke slowly, "I am so sorry, Trina." She saw a tear escape his eye and trickle down his cheek. He pulled both arms over his face and started to sob. His body was shaking from head to toe.

"Sorry? Sorry for what?" She put her hand on his shoulder. He didn't answer. He just lay there and sobbed.

"Shhh, Chad. It is okay. You are okay, and I am okay. Please, Chad, look at me."

His sobs shook his whole body. Katrina couldn't make him listen to her. He was so absorbed in sorrow. She didn't know what he was apologizing for. Finally, he removed one arm so she could see a portion of his face.

She put a hand on both sides of his face. "Chad, look at me," she quietly demanded. He slowly opened his eyes to focus on her. "What are you upset about?"

He looked at her as if she had grown a third eye. "I could not help you."

"But you did."

"I heard you screaming, Trina. I could not move. I could not get up. I must have passed out."

"What do you call shooting Silver Ghost then?" Katrina asked him.

Chad blinked a couple of times. With wonder in his voice, he asked, "I hit him then?"

She realized he didn't even know what had happened, so she filled him in. "Chad, you saved me from Silver Ghost's raping me." Puzzlement was written on his face. "You shot him before he could. You shot him dead."

Chad was stunned. "I could not see where I was shooting. I was not sure if I would hit you or him. I figured if I hit you, I would be doing you a favor. Better to have you dead than to have you raped by him. I thought we were both dead." He grabbed her to him and held her tight. "I thought I had lost you."

Katrina just lay in his arms. It felt good. She felt safe and cherished. She knew he was going to be okay. His blow to the head didn't make him loco, and he knew who he was. His memory was intact.

Chad had fallen back to sleep, so she decided to find something to fix him for supper. He would need some nourishment to build his strength back up.

She stood and stared at him. How much she wanted to really be his wife. How much she would relish him holding her regularly. How much she wished he could love her the way she loved him.

For two more days, Chad slept most of the time. Katrina fed him every three hours to help his body to heal physically and mentally.

The snow had since melted, and there hadn't been any more rain. Chad's horse, Streak, had come back the first day. He was a well-trained animal. They would have to ride together. Katrina had sent Silver Ghost's horse off. She wanted nothing around to remind either of them of him.

She would tell no one what had almost happened. A couple of times, she had woken in the night in a cold sweat. *The nightmares would go away over time,* she hoped. Each time she had woken, she was afraid she had disturbed Chad. Fortunately, he slept on. She didn't want him to have any guilt over what had almost happened. He had done everything in his power to protect her and in the end had saved her. She knew he would blame himself if he knew of the nightmares though. She needed to get all this behind her. She needed to go on with her life—the life she wanted very much to share with Chad.

They sat eating some venison Katrina was able to shoot. She hated killing the poor deer, but she wanted to make sure Chad got well, so she did what she had to do to help his body heal.

Chad hadn't said a whole lot. He had told her it hurt too much to talk, let alone chew. He was looking so much better. The black eyes were still there and probably would be for a week or so, but the swelling was almost gone.

"We probably should head for home soon, Trina."

"I do not want to rush you, Chad. We could wait a day or two more." The days seemed to drag on for her while he slept most of the time. It was better than for him to have complications.

"I think we could at least start out. I am not sure how far I will make it, but even an hour closer is closer."

Katrina couldn't argue with that logic. "Okay, we will head out after you finish your breakfast. Are sure you are up to it?"

Chad nodded slightly. "I think I will have a headache for the rest of my life, Trina. I will see the doc when we get you back home."

Katrina rose and started to pack up their belongings. "Chad, we will have to use one horse. The other is gone."

"Good by me," he mumbled, glad to have this whole Silver-Ghost episode out of the way.

"Sorry? I did not hear you." She thought he was complaining about riding with her. She felt a stab of pain in her chest. She didn't know how to show him she had fallen in love with him, and she didn't know what to do to get his love in return.

Katrina rolled up their bedding and tied it onto the back of his saddle. She helped him to mount Streak.

"I feel as weak as a newborn lamb," he sighed once he was on his horse.

"You just let me do the rest, Chad. I will get you home. As a matter of fact, we will ride into town first and have the doc take a look at your head, but if you need me to stop, just say so. I cannot read your mind to know when you have had enough for one day."

"Just let me lean on you, Trina, and we will go far together." He laid his head on her shoulder, and off they went at a very slow pace. She liked the sound of them going *far together*.

Chad was heavy. He was a big man, and she wasn't big enough to bear his weight for long. They had gone about two hours, and she had to have him put his head on the other shoulder. Her back was starting to kill her. She wasn't going to be able to last the whole day this way. It was definitely going to be a long ride the rest of the way. They would be lucky to be home in three days at this pace.

They stopped for lunch and Katrina was having muscle spasms in her neck and back.

She decided they had gone far enough for one day. She hoped he would be able to stay awake a little more tomorrow, so as to not have to lean on her as much.

Chad was so thankful to hear her say they had traveled far enough for one day. His head was pounding so hard that he could barely hear her talk. He laid down and fell asleep immediately.

Katrina was afraid she had pushed him too far too soon. She removed the saddle from Streak and walked down to the creek to get Chad some cool water. Streak was right on her heels. "You are a good boy." Katrina rubbed his neck as he drank from the stream.

She dipped a cloth in the water and placed it on Chad's forehead. He wasn't warm, but sometimes a cool cloth helped to make a headache feel better.

The nights were getting colder. They didn't have a lot to keep them warm except for each other. Katrina built a good-sized fire and had plenty of wood to keep it stoked through the night. She snuggled in next to Chad and fell asleep quickly.

Chad slept fitfully. He didn't know what kept waking him. He had to remind himself where he was when he woke. The fire was still burning when he opened his eyes. He didn't feel cold. It was Katrina that slept next to him. He liked that. He pulled her little rump up next to him. He held her tightly, not wanting to let her go. He was amazed how perfectly she fit to him. Then she tensed and made a noise that he remembered hearing while he was asleep and realized it was her that had kept waking him. She was having a dream. At first, he thought it was a good dream but could tell when it turned ugly. Her whole body tensed, and she screamed out. The scream was the same as the one he had heard when Silver Ghost had been straddling her. He knew what the dream was about and wanted so bad to be able to take the nightmare away.

"Shhh, Trina, I am here. I will not let anything happen to you again. I promise, baby. Shhhh." Chad held her tight and kept whispering to her until she calmed and went back into her sleep without the dream to haunt her. He didn't know how he was going to help her forget, but he vowed he would.

Katrina snuggled in tight. Then she rolled over and cuddled him from the front. She wrapped her arm around his waist and put one leg in between his legs. She was killing him. He could feel his body responding to her. He would truly make her his wife someday soon. This was another vow he intended to keep. In the meantime, he would control the urge to kiss her. As tempting as it was, he didn't think he could stop there, and then he would be trying to accomplish what Silver Ghost wasn't able to. He never intended to have Katrina that way. He wanted her more than anything right here and now, but more than that, he wanted her to feel safe. If he started mauling her every time, he felt like she would grow to hate him. She wouldn't believe him when he told her he loved her. She would think he was just trying to get on her good side to take advantage of her.

It took Chad a long time to be able to go back to sleep, and then it didn't last for long. He had slept so much lately he couldn't sleep at all now.

Chad was like a different person the next morning. When Katrina awoke, he was already up. She sat up and watched him move around the camp she had built the day before.

"Well, someone must be feeling better," she pointed out.

"As a matter of fact, I do feel much better. Thanks to the wonderful nurse I had."

Katrina blushed. She couldn't believe the difference one day had made for him. "Your hair is wet," she observed.

"That it is. Nothing like a cold dip to get the blood flowing, and believe me it is cold."

"Chad, you are telling me you went into that ice-cold water?" She was chilled just thinking about it.

"Yes, I am, and boy, do I feel good." He had his mischievous face back on. She had missed this side of him. He was so serious all the time, but at others, he was so much fun. She liked this side of him.

"Well, you look good. I think that cold water did you some good. It appears that your black eyes are clearing up almost overnight." She thought it would take at least days. Today, he was a little yellow under the eyes. If he continued to heal at this rate, he would be back to normal by the time they got home.

Chad brought her a plate with some fried fish on it. Katrina gladly accepted it. Their hands brushed when she reached for the plate. It was as if time stood still. They both just stared at each other. Katrina couldn't tear her eyes away. Chad's eyes were the deepest blue. She felt like she was drowning in the pools of his eyes.

Chad wanted to kiss her so bad right now. She was so appealing with her husky morning voice. She looked rested. She looked like she wanted to eat him as much as he wanted to eat her. What a morning meal she would make too.

Streak whinnied and brought them both out of the trance they had sunk into.

Chad cleared his throat and blinked at the same time. He stood abruptly, almost dumping her plate in her lap. "Yes, well, I thought you might be hungry."

"I am, Chad." Something about the way she said it made him believe she wasn't talking about the food. Chad was pleasantly surprised but realized he was reading too much into the moment.

Chad walked over and sat on a rock, eating his own fish. He was stabbing his fork at it as if he was angry. Katrina felt she had made him mad at her. What she didn't know was he was angry with himself for not expressing his feelings toward her. How could he though? He wasn't sure she really loved him, or if she just had a little-girl crush on him.

When Chad looked at her in the clothes she still wore from the Indian camp, she didn't look like a little girl. She looked like a full-grown woman. Her body had all the right curves, and her breasts were those of a woman, not a little girl or even a teenager. She truly was driving him crazy.

Katrina didn't know what his problem was. He was looking at her with a look she couldn't read. If she had to guess, she would say she'd made him mad about something. She had had enough of his fish. He could eat it if he wanted to, but she didn't want anything from him when he was going to look at her that way.

"I am going to clean up, then we can get on the road." She walked away in a huff.

Chad watched that backside walk away. Damn, she was a sight. It was all he could do to keep from devouring her. He needed to be careful, or his body was going to give him away. He should take another ice-cold dip. That would fix him. He got up and started packing up camp. He just needed to keep himself busy, to keep his mind on other things. He could do that. He just had to try harder.

Once they were on their way, Chad noticed that Katrina had been unusually quiet. She was riding in front of him. He had his arms around her holding the reins. "Are you okay?" he asked.

"Why would I not be?" she asked testily.

"You are just a little quiet. I was wondering if something was wrong. That is all." He could tell something was eating at her. She didn't reply, so he tried to start up a conversation. "What are you going to do when you get home?"

"Why?" She wasn't sure what he was asking.

"Well, about our marriage."

She didn't let him finish, "Do not worry, Chad. I am going to get it annulled." She knew he felt trapped, and that was not the way she wanted to be married to him. If he really wanted to marry her, he would have to ask her for himself. She knew it was a forced marriage, if you could call it that at all, but she was going to get a judge to do the annulment, so he could be sure she wasn't joking about this whole mess.

She knew this was probably the only way she would ever be married to Chad, but she cared for him too much to have him feeling trapped.

Chad wasn't happy that she hadn't let him finish his comment about the wedding vows they had repeated. Her words stung, and he wasn't so sure that she wasn't right about having it annulled. Obviously, she didn't want to be married to him after all. It all boiled down to her being a woman who didn't know her own mind. They were all the same in his book: stubborn, selfish, and little troublemakers.

That evening, they had decided to keep riding. They were just a few hours from town, and Chad really didn't want to sleep out in the open again. The temperature had been dropping every day, and he was afraid they would die from hypothermia.

Chad and Katrina finally reached town. "We can stay at Barbara's boarding house. I already have a room there. I am sure she can find a room for you. If not, you can have mine tonight, and I will get a room above the salon."

Katrina didn't want him to go to the salon; it might mean he would be sharing his bed with someone else—that someone else being a woman.

It was at least one in the morning by the time they reached Barbara's. Chad knew it was rude to disturb her at this hour, but he would explain it to her, and she would understand. He hoped.

Chad had let her in. He put his finger to his lips to hush Katrina. She was literally dragging her feet. As quiet as he tried to be, Barbara had gotten up when she heard the noise.

"Chad, ye frightened me. Where on earth have ye been? It's been almost three weeks since ye have been here. I almost rented your room out. I figured ye wasn't coming back."

Chad was trying to get a word in, but Barbara just kept chattering away, and then she noticed Katrina, "Oh, Chad, I won't be having ye bring women here. I don't allow such goings on in me place." Barbara couldn't believe the nerve of him. She had hoped that his staying here would allow them to get to know each other better. Then he disappeared then had the nerve to bring an imp with him when he returned.

Katrina was angry, but before she could say a word, Chad put his hand on her shoulder and spoke to Barbara. "Barbara, you remember Katrina Holt." Barbara's eyes grew like saucers.

"This can't be the little tomboy. Why, Chad, she's grown into a beauty." Then it dawned on her that this must be why he left the Holt ranch to begin with. A stab of jealousy hit Barbara looking at Katrina. Barbara came to terms that she wouldn't stand a chance in occupying some of Chad's time. He definitely had his brand on Katrina Holt.

Katrina shrugged Chad's hand off her shoulder. These two were talking as if she weren't even in the room. She could tell Barbara had an eye for Chad, and she was seething. "Excuse me, but I am tired. If you could show me to the room, I would like to go to sleep."

Barbara was a little confused but not for long. Chad spoke up. "Barbara, we need a room for Katrina to sleep in. If you do not have an extra, I can go to the salon."

"Oh, that won't be necessary, Chad. I have a fold out in thee parlor." Barbara was elated to see they weren't intending to share a room. She might have a chance after all. "Katrina, ye follow me. Chad, I'll be down in a minute."

Katrina followed her but not before she stuck her tongue at her back. When Chad burst out laughing, Katrina was mortified that he had seen her act so childishly.

The room was cozy to say the least. Chad had a few of his personal items around the room. Barbara watched her look around so adoringly. She knew that Katrina was in love with Chad, but was Chad in love with Katrina? Barbara intended to find out.

"The bath is at the end of the hall if ye be wanting to clean up some," Barbara offered.

"I am too tired tonight, maybe in the morning." Katrina frowned and yawned.

"Good night to ye then." Barbara closed the door.

When Barbara went downstairs, she found Chad in the parlor. He was oversized for her little furniture. He was oversized for any furniture. "She be all settled in." Barbara was standing with her hands behind her, which accented her breast. Chad had to pull his eyes up to hers when she talked.

He had been too long without a woman, and being in such close proximity with Katrina this last week had only added to his need.

"You know, Barbara, I just might need to visit the salon after all."

Barbara smiled. She knew her nightgown was revealing, and she herself was on fire for him. She just needed to figure out how to get him to come to her bed. She approached him. Standing in front of him, she ran her fingers through his hair. "Chad, there's nothing there that isn't here. I have whiskey and a bed for ye." Her voice was so seductive he was almost tempted.

His face was in her breast. Well, not exactly in them, but he was nose level because he was sitting, and he could smell her sweet perfume. She was intoxicating.

Then he heard himself say, "I am married." Boy, if that wasn't like throwing water on a fire. They both shook their heads to snap out of the dream they had both weaved. Barbara jumped back as if she had been burned.

"What did ye say?" Her shock was instantly recognizable.

Chad couldn't believe he blurted that out. He could have had it all, not at the cost of losing Katrina though. And he knew where this little rendezvous would end up. He couldn't gamble Katrina finding out. He needed a cold shower. He needed to make love to Katrina. He just wasn't sure how he was going to achieve that.

Barbara was still waiting for an answer. "It is not a real marriage, you see. We were married by the tribe leader. Katrina does not see it as a real marriage anyway. She is having it annulled tomorrow."

Barbara could hear the disappointment in Chad's voice. She didn't like to play games with people's emotions, but this was a man she would be willing to hold her tongue for. If he hadn't figured out that Katrina was in love with him and he in love with her, she wouldn't be the one to point out the obvious.

"I am sorry, Barbara. I did not mean for this to get out of control. I will be back in the morning."

Chad headed out the door. Barbara realized he probably didn't even know he was in love with Katrina. Some men could be so stupid.

Katrina had been tucked in bed when she realized she hadn't told Chad good night. She had walked quietly down the stairs. She stopped dead in her tracks. What she saw made her blood run cold. Chad had his hands on Barbara's hips with his face in her breast, while Barbara ran her hands through his hair. Her head was down as if she was kissing his head.

Katrina ran upstairs and closed the door quietly. She threw herself on the bed. "How could you, Chad?" she sobbed. "I hate you. I hate you." She hit his pillow with each word. She couldn't believe she had let him get to her. She vowed to never let another man under her skin, but as much as she tried, she couldn't stop crying. She cried herself to sleep.

Chad sat at the salon for what seemed like hours. He drank until he could feel his head stop aching. Maureen was sitting across the table from him. She was just waiting for him to drop, then she was going to have him carried up to her room and put him to bed—in her bed. Chad wasn't in much of a talking mood tonight. She hadn't seen him since he came in and drank away the last woman. She didn't know if he was still trying to drown the same one out or a new one. Boy, she wished she could be the one he was trying to drown out.

Maureen got up and took his hand. "Come on, Chad. I have a bed for you to rest in."

Chad looked straight through her, not seeing her at all. He got up and followed her. When he saw the bed, he fell face-first into it. Maureen tried, but she couldn't budge him. He was too big. It was late, and she was exhausted. Obviously, she wasn't going to be having a taste of this cowboy tonight, so she just removed his boots because without his cooperation there was nothing else coming off this cowboy. She undressed herself and climbed into bed next to him. Maybe in the morning, she could get his cooperation.

Barbara was in her kitchen when Katrina came down the stairs the following morning. Katrina wasn't about to stay any longer than she had to. "Thank you for the bed, Barbara." Katrina's thank you was kind of cold.

Barbara turned to see Katrina was still in the outfit she had arrived in. "Don't ye have any clothes other than the Indian dress, Katrina?"

"No, I am afraid I do not. I wanted to see the judge for some personal business." Katrina said the last part quickly, "But I need to go home and get some clothes first."

Barbara was more than willing to help Katrina set Chad free. "Why don't I loan ye a dress? I'm sure I have something that would fit ye."

Katrina didn't know what to say.

"After all, Katrina, it's such a long way to go just for a change of clothes. Really, I don't mind. Ye could return the dress anytime."

The two of them went up to Barbara's room. Katrina looked around to see if there was any evidence of Chad sleeping in there with Barbara last night. Earlier when she had gone downstairs, there had been no evidence of him sleeping in the parlor.

Katrina asked, "Where is Chad this morning?"

"Well, he needed to take care of some personal business." Barbara didn't imply that it was last night. Let Katrina think what she wanted.

Katrina was feeling really low. She hadn't known Chad had a relationship going with Barbara. She had hoped he would want to marry her on his own terms. She had hoped by releasing him from a bond he hadn't asked for that he would respect her for caring about him so much that he would fall in love with her. After seeing the way he was with Barbara, she realized she had nothing to offer Chad. Barbara had everything. Katrina wanted to hurry up and get the annulment. She needed to get away from Chad and his Barbara.

Once Katrina was all decked out in one of Barbara's pretty dresses, she headed over to find the judge. She was walking down Main Street when she saw Chad come out of the salon with a woman on his arm. The woman was pretty. Chad didn't seem to mind that she was rubbing her voluptuous body on him. Then she watched as Chad bent down to give the woman a soft kiss on the cheek. He whispered something in her ear, and she giggled. Katrina had seen enough. She slipped into the mercantile. She continued to watch through the window and was appalled when Chad smacked the woman on the bottom, sending her back inside.

"Of all the nerve." Katrina seethed. First, he cheated on her with Barbara, and now he was cheating on Barbara with the salon girl. Katrina was seeing a side of Chad she had never seen before. It was one she didn't like at all. He was a two-timing scoundrel.

"Who you spyin' on?" Mrs. Jenkins startled Katrina as she approached from behind to look out the window.

"Oh, you scared me." Katrina jumped then backed away from the window.

Mrs. Jenkins continued to look out the window. The only one she saw on the street was Chad. She was talking to Katrina as she continued to look out the window. "I never saw you at the Thorn's barn dance." Then she turned to Katrina. "I thought we had a deal about the dress. I was disappointed when you did not show up."

With everything that had been going on, she had completely forgot about the dress.

Katrina looked mortified. "Oh, Mrs. Jenkins, I am so sorry. We had a terrible accident out at the ranch, and I was seeing to the recovery of the injured party. Then I went on a short trip. I have not even been home yet from the trip. My mother does not even know that I am okay." Katrina was sobbing as she was rambling on. "And now I need to find the judge. Oh, Mrs. Jenkins, please forgive me."

Mrs. Jenkins could tell Katrina was overly excited about a lot of things, but the one thing that caught her attention while she was rambling on was the need for the judge.

Mrs. Jenkins interrupted Katrina, "Dear, dear, what on earth do you need a judge for?"

Katrina looked at her shamefacedly. "I need to get an annulment."

"A what?" Mrs. Jenkins being shocked would be an understatement. "Who on earth did you marry?"

Katrina looked at her with big watery eyes then burst into tears again. "Chad Miles." She sobbed, frustrated at herself for crying again. She seemed to be crying every time she turned around lately, and it was always because of Chad Miles. She hated him for making her so miserable.

Mrs. Jenkins was confused. "Katrina dear, I thought you were in love with Chad. Why on earth after you got married to him would you want to annul the wedding?"

"Because he is a scoundrel."

"Well, you must be talking about another Chad. The Chad I know is far from a scoundrel."

"He is, I tell you. Last night, he was being sweet with Barbara, and this morning he was being sweet with a salon girl." Mrs. Jenkins was a little shocked to hear what Katrina was saying.

"Did you see this *being sweet* with your own eyes, or is it the word of someone else?"

"No, I saw it for myself. Both incidences."

"Well, that does make a difference. Are you going to let him go that easy, or are you going to fight back?" Mrs. Jenkins had an idea.

"What do you mean?" Katrina had stopped crying finally.

"I mean if you are jealous of him with other women, maybe, just maybe, two can play at this game."

"I do not understand. What game are you talking about?"

"Katrina, is there any possibility that Chad might return your feelings?"

"I might have thought so at one time, but he was forced into this marriage, and he is angry about it."

When Katrina said *forced*, Mrs. Jenkins thought of the wrong thing immediately. "Katrina dear, are you with child?"

Katrina jumped back as if she had been burned. "*No!*"

"Do not be alarmed, child. Now I am the one that does not understand. How was he forced?"

"I had to choose between him or someone else. Neither of us was given a choice. Rather than me have to choose, he chose for me. He was just trying to be loyal to our family. He knew I did not want to marry the other guy, so he stepped in. I told him I would get it annulled as soon as we got home."

Mrs. Jenkins's mind was reeling. Most men needed a little help understanding their own feelings. If Chad did care for Katrina, and Mrs. Jenkins couldn't think of any reason why he wouldn't, then he might need a little help in seeing how he felt, and the little green-eyed monster of jealousy was sure to pop up if he did care.

"Well, there is another barn dance tomorrow night. You could go in the dress I gave you and dance with all the other men. If he is upset by it, then you know he returns your feelings. Are you willing to give it a try?"

Katrina was still a little confused. "You mean I should try to make him jealous?"

"Yes, dear, that is exactly what I mean. Some men do not know their own mind. They have to be shown what is best for them."

Katrina felt that if any man knew his own mind, it was Chad, but rather than stay home while everyone else went to the dance, she would go and try to have fun. "What if Chad is there with someone? What if he dances with someone else? Then I will be the one jealous and hurt."

"We will not let that happen. You need to learn to hide those feelings. Tomorrow we work on making him see the light. You have already seen it."

"Are you sure this will work?"

"Trust me, Katrina. You have your ma do your hair nice, and you wear that dress, and every man in the place will be fightin' over a dance with you."

Katrina felt better. She would win Chad over if it were the last thing she did.

"Now you hold off on that annulment. We will see if Chad wants it or not."

CHAPTER TEN

Chad had gone back to Barbara's home to fetch Katrina and take her home. When he had arrived, Barbara shared with him that she went to seek out the judge for her annulment. Chad was angry. She was really going to go through with it. He wasn't sure how to change her mind; all he knew was that he did want to change her mind.

When he'd woken up this morning in Maureen's bed, he was horrified to realize that that was where he had spent the night. He couldn't remember how he had gotten there, but he was, and there was no excuse. Maureen was as happy as a cackling hen this morning. Chad couldn't get out of there soon enough. If nothing else, he needed to stay married to Katrina just to stay safe from all the women trying to tie him down.

Barbara was no different this morning. She definitely wanted him to stay on but in her room, not his.

"I need to go," Chad informed Barbara.

"Must ye, Chad. She's made her choice. It's obvious she wants out of the marriage to ye."

Barbara's words hurt. Maybe it wasn't too late. Chad repeated, "I need to go." He stormed out of the house. Barbara watched him go, feeling as if she was losing the battle.

Chad was headed back to Main Street on Streak. He would look for Katrina at the courthouse. As he was going down Main Street, he saw Katrina coming out of the mercantile. "Katrina!" he hollered out to her.

She stopped at the edge of the wood sidewalk. The sun was shining, so she had to cover her eyes with her hand to look up at Chad.

She looked so pretty in the dress. Chad wasn't sure where she had gotten it. He didn't know if she had gotten her paperwork for the annulment, and he didn't have the guts to ask her. He didn't want to know. "Do you need a lift home, Trina?"

She hated him. Sometimes he could be so sweet, but she had to remember that he was a scoundrel. "I think I would be better off walking. Unfortunately, I do not have the proper attire, so yes, I would like a ride home."

He could tell she was ticked off about something. Right now, he wanted to get her home to her ma so that she knew Katrina was safe. He would be sure to ask her what the matter was on the ride home, once he had her in the saddle.

Chad got down and lifted her up into the saddle so that she could ride sidesaddle with the dress on. He climbed on behind her, and they headed home.

The ride was quiet at first. They saw a few people on the road home and would stop and talk for a few minutes to each one, just to be neighborly.

One couple they ran across was Sue and Jeff. Sue spoke first, "Why, you two make a grand couple!" she praised.

Katrina felt her cheeks burn. She wished it were true—the couple part—but they weren't.

"How you doing, Jeff?" Chad asked.

"Will not complain, Chad." Jeff reached over and rubbed Sue's tummy. "We have us a babe, Chad." Jeff beamed. He was the proud father-to-be.

Katrina felt a stab of jealousy. "Congratulations, Sue. You do have quite the glow about you."

"Thank you, Katrina. I could not be happier. Will we see you at the dance tomorrow night?" Sue was asking both of them.

"I will be there, but I cannot speak for Chad."

Chad was surprised that Katrina even knew about it. He had heard talk of it last night in the salon. He wondered how Katrina found out. He had intended to ask her to attend the dance with him, but the way she just put it was as if she already had been asked to the dance by someone else.

Chad wasn't about to let that happen. "Well, if my *wife* is attending the dance, I think I should be there." Chad knew he struck a nerve with Katrina and shocked the other couple.

"What?" Sue was asking.

"You are married?" Jeff was asking at the same time.

"Chad!" Katrina jabbed him in the ribs with her elbow. She was furious.

Rather than try to explain himself to everyone, he covered Katrina's mouth with his and gave her a kiss that left no argument from anyone. At first, Katrina fought him. She was so angry with him for all his indiscretions, but the kiss was more than she could stand. She had wanted him to kiss her more than anything. She wanted so badly for him to love her. This kiss was curling her toes.

When he pulled away, he whispered against her lips, "Do not say a word."

Katrina was taken aback. Why would Chad tell them that she was his wife? They said their goodbyes and headed home again.

Katrina couldn't wait until they were out of earshot, then she turned on Chad. "Why would you do that?"

"Do what?" He wasn't sure if she was asking about the kiss or that he had told them they were married.

"Do not play innocent with me, Chad. If we do not tell anyone we are married, then it will make the annulment go easier. Do you think?" More than anything, she wanted to let Chad off the hook. She couldn't think straight right now. His kiss had meant everything to her, but to him, it was probably just a stupid kiss. He seemed to like kissing a lot of girls. Let's see. Three different women in two days. He was a scoundrel.

Chad had been looking for any reason to wrap his lips around hers again. It seemed like the perfect reason—just to shut her up. He knew he had shocked her by telling Jeff they were married. He didn't know why he blurted it out. Yes, he did, damn it. He wanted everyone to know she was his wife.

Her words kept haunting him about it being easier to get the annulment if no one knew. He didn't want to make it easier, so maybe it was the best way to hold on to her. If he told a lot of people they were married, maybe she would leave it be, and they could stay married.

"Do you think?" Katrina repeated her question after he didn't answer right away.

They were almost to the ranch. Chad needed to know if she had seen the judge. "Did you get the paperwork straightened out, Katrina?"

His words stung her. He did want her to seek the judge after all. "Chad, you confuse me." She was mad again. "Do not worry. I have everything taken care of."

He never got his answers and neither did she as they rode into the compound.

Everyone at the ranch had just sat down for the noon meal when someone yelled out that there was a rider approaching.

Evelyn dropped the spoon she was using to ladle the beans onto the plates and ran to the porch. She went to her knees when she saw Katrina and Chad together, safe and sound. She hadn't been sleeping or eating well. She had been so worried about the both of them.

Katrina jumped off Streak and ran into her mother's arms. They held each other down on their knees. Both of them were crying. "I am okay, Ma. I am okay," Katrina kept repeating.

All standing around, watching their exchange of love, were teary-eyed.

Katrina helped her mother to her feet. Somehow her mother had aged in the short time Katrina had been away. It dawned on Katrina that this whole ordeal had taken a toll on her mother as well, and why would it not? Katrina loved her mother so much. She felt so lucky to have someone who cared about her so much.

"Oh, Mama." Katrina wrapped her mother in her arms again. "Let me take you inside. Everything is going to be okay now. I promise."

Everyone hovered around Katrina and her mother. Chad watched as they all walked into the house. Bo approached him and slapped Chad on the back with a bear hug. "Thanks for bringing her home safely. Ma has been beside herself."

Chad sat on the steps of the porch. "Bo, I have something to tell you."

Bo sat next to him. Chad's voice was serious, so Bo gave him his full attention.

"Katrina and I are married."

Bo hooted with joy, but before he could express too much happiness, Chad spoke again. "She wants to get it annulled, Bo."

"But why? I could have sworn that she was in love with you. Does she want to go back to the Indian?"

"No!" Chad was abrupt. "That is not the problem. He is dead anyway."

Bo was shocked by the news. "What happened?"

"Bo, it is such a long story. It seems like years have gone by in the last several weeks." Chad rested his elbows on his knees and rested his head in the palms of his hands.

"Do you want the annulment, Chad?"

"Hell, no."

"Have you told her?"

"She will not have it any other way. She feels I was forced into the marriage. I would not let her marry Silver Ghost, so I stepped in, and she wants to repay me for helping her by helping me to be free again."

"You need to tell her or show her you do not want the annulment."

"I am not sure how to go about it. She can be so stubborn when she sets her mind to something."

Bo put his hand on Chad's shoulder and squeezed. "Follow your heart, Chad. You will not go wrong." Then he added, "By the way, she is not the only stubborn one around here." Bo met Chad's eyes head-on and raised an eyebrow, daring Chad to argue that one.

Chad had to chuckle at that. Chad cupped Bo's hand and squeezed back. "Thanks, Bo. I have some thinking to do. I will see you around." Chad got up to leave.

"Please come in for the noon meal. Ma will want to thank you herself."

"Thanks, Bo, but no. Maybe I will see you at the barn dance tomorrow night."

"I will be there with my best dancin' boots on." Bo pulled Chad back into a hug. "I for one will not be disappointed to have you as one of the family, Chad. Thanks for all that you did for Katrina and Ma."

Chad mounted Streak. "I was doing it for me. I have become a little selfish when it comes to that sister of yours."

"I am not sorry to hear that, Chad. See you tomorrow."

Bo watched as Chad rode away. He turned to see Katrina come out the kitchen door.

With worry, she asked, "Where is Chad going? He did not even say goodbye." Her feelings were hurt. She didn't want him to leave. He belonged here, always.

"He said he would see us at the dance tomorrow." Bo wrapped an arm over Katrina's shoulder as he ushered her back into the house.

Katrina sat at the table with everyone for the noon meal. It was déjà vu. She had lived this dream once before when she had come home the first time. She answered all the questions and told of Chad shooting Silver Ghost. She left out a few details. Bo had noticed, especially the one of them being married. He decided to sit back and watch this play out.

The following day seemed to drag for Katrina. Although she had plenty to do to get ready for the dance, she wanted it to hurry up. She missed Chad and wanted to tell him. She didn't want to play games. She would give him his annulment and then hope with all the hope she could muster that Chad would ask her to marry him on his own.

Evelyn had helped her wash and curl her hair. They had put it up into a beautiful bun on her head with tendrils falling on her shoulders. The dress required a little adjustment to the waist. Katrina had lost some weight on this last adventure, and the dress seemed to hang on her. Luckily for her, her mother was able to take it in in all the proper places.

Katrina and her mother sat and talked the whole day while preparing food for the dance. She had never felt closer to her mother.

In the late afternoon, everyone gathered in the compound. The whole ranch was to attend the barn dance. They were going to ride together. Bo had had the buckboard cleaned up so that Katrina and his ma would arrive in style.

Evelyn had a few of the men help her put the food she and Katrina had prepared throughout the day at the back of the buckboard.

Everyone was waiting outside, so Bo walked into the house to holler for Katrina to let her know that all was ready. Before he got her name out, she walked out of her bedroom. Bo just stood there, shocked to say the least.

Katrina looked up to see his expression. This was her brother for goodness sakes, but she turned three shades of red anyway.

"Katrina darlin'." Bo whistled. "You do not want me to have any fun tonight, do you?"

Confused, she asked, "What do you mean, Bo? Of course, I want you to have fun. I want everyone to have fun."

She was fidgeting with the bag she was carrying to match the dress she wore. Bo had never seen such a vision. The dress was like a glove on a perfect body. If she wasn't his own sister, he might have to be chasing her himself. He shook his head and cleared his throat. "Katrina darlin', I will be too busy fightin' off three-fourths of this town tonight. The fourth I will not have to worry about will be the boys under ten years old and the old coots over eighty. Other than that, you will probably not sit for a second tonight. I sure hope you got yourself a good pair of dancin' shoes."

Katrina was warmed by the compliment. She lifted her skirt to show him she still wore her cowboy boots, and he hooted with laughter.

Bo walked over and gave her a hug. "In case I have not told you lately, sis, I sure love you. I pray you will never change. You are perfect the way you are."

Katrina's eyes filled up with tears for two reasons. The words her brother just shared with her was the first time she could remember him ever saying he loved her, and the second was because Chad obviously didn't find her to be perfect.

"Now none of that allowed," Bo said as he took out his handkerchief to dab her eyes for her.

Katrina took the handkerchief from him and blew her nose. When she went to hand it back to Bo, he politely said, "You keep it." Katrina looked at the expression on his face, and they both burst out laughing.

They headed outside, and as the door closed behind them, all the men in the compound started whistling and hooting catcalls.

Again, Katrina was taken aback. This kind of attention was new to her. Not that she didn't like it, but she just didn't know how to respond. Would she ignore it or acknowledge the fact that they were paying her a compliment? She decided to acknowledge and curtsied.

"Can I have the first dance?" one of the men hollered out.

"No, choose me, Katrina. He has three left feet," another hollered out.

"Oh, give up, men. She has always had a fancy for me!" another exaggerated as he elbowed his way to the front of the other men. Bo winked at Katrina when she looked over to him for help, and they both laughed to see it was Smitty, every bit of one hundred years old.

"Guess that will be nine-tenths," Bo whispered as he pushed Katrina toward the buckboard. "Meaning, the old men will be chasing your skirt as well." They both laughed.

Evelyn felt such pride over her daughter's beauty. Her father would have been so proud of his only daughter.

Katrina was on cloud nine all the way to the dance. She couldn't wait to see Chad. She hoped that he would be pleased by her attire, as everyone else seemed to be.

The music was already playing by the time they arrived. Everything looked so festive. Katrina realized that this was truly the first dance she had really wanted to attend. She had attended all the others because her mother had told her she was expected to show up. But she had never worn a dress to any of them, and she had never danced except with her brothers. A nervousness was taking hold of her. She looked to her mother. "Ma, I don't know what to do."

129

Evelyn squeezed her hand. "Just have fun, dear. The evening will progress just fine."

Everyone pitched in to help carry the vittles over to the tables. The tables were already full to excess, so Bo and James grabbed another to set up in the line. People were still arriving, so they had made a good choice because they were all carrying dishes of wonderful-looking food.

Katrina looked around to see if she could find Chad. He wasn't out on the dance floor, he wasn't in the food line, and he wasn't by the beer tree. He didn't appear to be there at all.

Someone tapped Katrina on the shoulder. She turned to find Alex Shoemaker. "Could I have this dance?"

Katrina didn't want to be rude, so she accepted, and that's where it all began for her. The invitations didn't stop. Sometimes she would be dancing with someone, and someone else would break in. It got to the point that she started looking for someone to rescue her. She hadn't seen Chad anywhere.

They had been there at least two hours, and he hadn't seemed to arrive yet.

Bo was having a wonderful time listening to all the young women talk about Katrina out of jealousy.

"There is no way that is Katrina Holt!" one had exclaimed.

"She does not have hair like that," another chimed in.

"She is not pretty at all. That girl, whoever she is, is really pretty," proclaimed yet another.

Bo walked over to the one that had proclaimed his sister pretty and asked her to dance.

Chad had been sitting out of sight ever since the Holt family arrived. He knew Katrina was a beautiful flower that had blossomed into a perfect rose, but the sight of her took his breath away. She was stunning, and she was his for the moment at least.

He didn't want to ruin her fun with the foul mood he was in. The jealousy of her dancing with all those men was eating him up. He had a mind to proclaim her as his wife so that they would all stay away, but that would make her mad at him, and the last thing he wanted to do was make her mad.

He had decided he would wait out most of the evening before he asked her to dance. He was afraid that if he danced with her sooner, he wouldn't be willing to share her with anyone for the rest of the night. As a matter of fact, he was sure that once he danced with her, no one else was going to have a turn.

This hiding out was too much for him though. Maybe he should just ask someone else to dance to keep himself busy until the right time for him to burst in came. Whenever that was, he wasn't sure, but it would have to be soon, or he was going to explode with jealousy.

Chad looked up to see Barbara approaching him. She was a beauty, no doubt, but she didn't seem as beautiful ever since Katrina started overtaking his thoughts every moment, every second of the day.

Barbara asked, "Chad, would ye care to dance with an ol lady?"

"Old? I do not think so, Barbara. You are one of the prettiest girls here tonight," Chad answered honestly. "And yes, I would like to dance."

Katrina looked up just in time to see Chad and Barbara enter the dance floor, holding hands. *So that is where he has been all night,* she thought. How could he not care about her feelings? She loved him so much, and he didn't seem to care. Well, she was going to do as Mrs. Jenkins had coached her to do. She would try to make Chad jealous of her. But if he really liked Barbara, then she would just be making a fool of herself. All of a sudden, she didn't feel like dancing anymore.

"If you will excuse me, Jared, I need to get something to drink. My throat is parched."

"I will go with you, Ms. Katrina."

"Oh, that will not be necessary, Jared. I think I will sit out a few with my ma," she excused herself as politely as she could.

Jared walked her to the side of the dance floor then found another partner.

Katrina approached her ma and sat down with a huff.

"Tired, honey?"

"A little," Katrina admitted.

"Well, you ought to be. You have not stopped since we got here. Are you ready to eat?" Evelyn watched as Katrina watched Chad out on the dance floor.

"No, Mama, I am not hungry." Katrina pouted.

A young man approached and asked Katrina to dance. She politely explained she was famished and would dance with him after she ate.

"That is funny. I thought you said you were not hungry," her mother reminded her with a laugh in her voice. "It is a good thing your daddy ain't here, Katrina."

"Why would you say that, Mama?"

"Because he would be pulling those young men away from you. He would be asking for a proposal before he would allow them to dance with you."

Katrina knew her ma was just teasing, and it felt good to be told in so many ways how pretty she was. She just wished Chad thought so.

Katrina turned her back to the dance floor. She couldn't watch Chad and Barbara dance together. She felt really depressed and wanted to go home.

"Ma, how late do you want to stay?"

"You cannot possibly be ready, Katrina. This dance will go for hours yet."

Katrina felt a tap on her shoulder. She turned to see Bo bowing gallantly. "May I have this dance, fair maiden?" he asked, bowing all the way to his boots.

Katrina giggled. Bo always had a way of making her feel better. "You may. Thank you, Bo."

The song was a fast square dance where you changed partners over and over again. When Katrina bowed in front of Chad, her heart stopped.

Chad's hand was around her waist as he swung her around. "You sure look pretty tonight, my little Trina."

Katrina's heart swelled. "Thank you, Chad. You are looking mighty handsome yourself."

Chad squeezed her tighter, but it didn't get to last long because they had to change partners again.

No matter where Katrina was on the dance floor, she kept her eyes on Chad. What was warming was that he had done the same until they came together again.

"I would like the next slow dance with you, Trina."

"You may have it," she answered, looking him straight in the eye.

"I want the rest of the slow dances with you, Trina."

She couldn't tell him he could have all of them because they had to separate again but continued watching each other. When they came to each other again, she stated, "You got here late!"

He smiled down at her. "I have been here all along watching my wife have the time of her life with all kinds of partners, Trina."

She was shocked at his words. She hadn't seen him anywhere, and she had really looked. She couldn't respond because they were separated again.

That dance ended, and another fast dance was starting. Katrina had a swarm of men around her. Chad didn't care anymore. She promised him the next slow dance. She could have all the fast dances with everyone else, but the slow dances were for him and him alone.

Katrina continued to dance, and Chad walked over to Evelyn. They hadn't really had the chance to talk, and she stood to give him a big hug.

"How is my hero doing tonight?" she asked as she hugged him tight.

"Now there is no reason for that. I would have walked to the ends of the earth to find her, Evelyn."

They both sat down, and Chad continued to talk. "I want you to know that I intend to make her my wife, Evelyn."

Evelyn's face lit up with happiness. "Chad, if you're asking my permission, you have it."

"Well, that is good because she is already my wife." Chad had to laugh at the flabbergasted expression on Evelyn's face.

"What? She never said a word to me, Chad."

"I know. She is in denial, but I am not. She is my wife, and I intend to keep it that way."

"I do not think I understand, Chad." Worry and confusion both furrowed her brow.

Chad explained to whole story to Evelyn. He left a few of the gory details out. He wasn't sure what Katrina had told everyone at the noon meal, but he was sure she had spared her mother some of the detail so as not to worry her.

Two fast songs had played while Chad told Evelyn the whole story. When he realized that the tempo had changed, he looked up to see Katrina in the arms of yet another young pup.

"If you will excuse me, this number belongs to me." Chad stood to leave.

"Of course, Chad. Go claim what is yours," Evelyn told him.

Chad liked the sound of that. *Claim what is mine.* Chad approached the couple on the dance floor. Just as he was to reach them, Maureen grabbed his hand.

"Dance with me, Chad," she begged.

Chad looked at Maureen. She was looking so pretty tonight.

"Please, Chad, you have not asked me to dance all night. I have been waiting, very patiently, I might add."

Chad didn't have the heart to tell her no. Maureen had always been nice to him, and although those days were over, one little dance wouldn't hurt.

"Okay, Maureen, but just one dance."

Chad took Maureen in his arms, and she snuggled right in. She knew that he was headed for the little blonde, but she couldn't let that happen. Everyone had been taken into that little blonde's spell tonight, but she wasn't going to let Chad fall under it.

Maureen looked up to see Chad watching the girl. She couldn't take it anymore. "Who is she, Chad?"

"Who is who?" he asked not realizing that the expression on his face said it all.

"The girl that everyone is fightin' over to dance with," Maureen answered with sarcasm.

Chad chuckled. "You must mean Katrina." That was all that he offered her at first.

"What is so special about her? I mean, she is pretty and all, but why is everyone so taken in with her?"

Chad chuckled again. "I cannot answer for everyone else, but I know why she has caught my fancy."

"You are not goin' to be taken in by her too, are you, Chad? She is too young for you, Chad. You need a real woman."

Chad put his hands on Maureen's shoulders and pushed her out far enough that he could look her in the eye. "Maureen, I am taken in by her because she is my wife."

When Maureen's jaw hit the floor, Chad burst out laughing. It felt good to laugh. It felt good to tell people that he was married to Katrina. Not so much because it never seemed to not shock someone but because it felt good to claim her.

"Now if you will excuse me, I want this next dance with my wife." Chad left Maureen standing there as he approached Katrina again.

Katrina wasn't one bit happy with Chad right now. He had told her that he was going to have the next slow dance with her, but no, he had chosen to dance with someone else, and she could hear him laughing behind her. And if she wasn't mistaken, it was the same woman that was all over him in front of the salon yesterday morning. She was not happy at all with Chad Miles at this moment, so she was taken aback when her partner backed away from her and she saw Chad standing behind him.

"I believe the lady promised me the rest of the slow dances," she heard Chad telling her partner.

"I am afraid you are mistaken, buddy. This dance is mine," Katrina heard her partner say.

"No! I am afraid you are mistaken, lad. The lady belongs to me."

As much as Katrina loved to hear Chad say those words, she didn't like the way he was trying to bully his way into this dance. He had his chance and chose to dance with the woman with breast big enough for three women. Katrina couldn't help notice how the woman kept rubbing herself all over Chad. The whole time, Chad had had a smile on his face. Well, he could wait until the next slow dance; she already had a partner.

"Chad, do not be ridiculous. I do not belong to anyone. Now run along and wait your turn."

Chad was stunned. Was she letting all this attention go to her head? Well, that was fine. He wasn't going to beg for her attention. "I will not ask again, Trina," Chad stated matter-of-factly, giving her one last opportunity to move into his arms.

"Chad, you are being rude. You may ask me to dance the next slow dance."

The young man took Katrina back into his arms. Looking over his shoulder, he said to Chad, "You heard the lady. She has made her decision, and you are not it." He gloated.

His words stung both Katrina and Chad. She hadn't meant for Chad to feel she didn't want to dance with him at all, but who did he think he was anyway? He didn't own her after all.

Chad had had enough fun for one night. Katrina was acting like she was a free woman. Maybe in her eyes she was but not in his. She was his wife. He didn't know if he should make a scene or just leave. He decided on the latter.

Barbara had watched as Katrina refused Chad's offer to dance. That had to hurt. All the better for her though. She would help to mend the wound. She saw Chad start to head back to her place, so she ran after him.

Katrina continued to dance with her partner until the end of the song. She thanked him and went in search for Chad. She did want to dance with him. As a matter of fact, she wanted to dance the rest of the dances with him.

Katrina ran into Bo. "Have you seen Chad?" she asked innocently.

Bo looked around and pointed down the road. "It looks like he is leavin'."

"Leaving?" Katrina asked and looked in the direction Bo was pointing. Then she saw Chad and Barbara walking arm in arm. "Well." Katrina stomped her foot. "How could he?"

Bo looked from one to the other and was a little confused himself. "Sis, you should go find out what is going on? Or do you want me to ask him?"

"No, let him go," Katrina spit out with so much anger. She was seeing green from that little green-eyed monster named jealousy. "I am ready to go home, Bo. Are you ready?"

"Any time, sis. Go collect Ma."

Bo knew that he was dealing with the two most stubborn people he could ever meet. If they ever did get their act together, they would either have the most passionate love for each other or they would destroy one another. He hoped for the passion. They both needed such a love. It was just a matter of the meeting of the minds and hearts. He might have to intervene a little. He would give it some thought.

In the meantime, Maureen watched as Chad left with Barbara instead of Katrina and was quite confused. If he truly was married to Katrina, why was he not leaving with her? This whole thing was a big fat lie on Chad's part as far as she was concerned. Maybe she could persuade him back to her bed again after all. She vowed to give it another try. Obviously Katrina didn't look at the relationship as Chad did. Maureen definitely had a thing for Chad and would use every charm in her body to get him to see she could be a good woman for him.

The ride home for Katrina was miserable. This evening didn't go as she had hoped it would. As a matter of fact, it was a disaster. She had never really gotten to dance with Chad other than the square dance where they ran into each other here and there, and he left with another woman—a woman he had been having an affair with all along. Well, Katrina was not going to be made a laughingstock. She would go seek out that judge tomorrow and get that annulment. She would not cry. She would not cry.

Evelyn spoke up when the silence was too much to bear. "I kind of figured that Chad would be escorting you home tonight, Katrina. What happened?"

Katrina snapped at her ma but immediately felt apologetic. "He left with the woman he has been having an affair with." A second later, she said, "I am sorry, Mama. I think I have a broken heart."

"Katrina, that does not make any sense to me." Evelyn was about to tell her the conversation she had had with Chad. But Katrina was going to be too stubborn to listen tonight.

"Well, he did leave with her, and I do not want to talk about it anymore. It is over. I have learned my lesson about Chad. He is nothing more than a rotten, cheatin' scoundrel." Her tone sounded like she was done talking about it, so Evelyn decided to just keep her thoughts to herself. This definitely had to be a misunderstanding somehow.

Bo just listened as they rode along. It did seem as if Katrina had a point about Chad having an affair with Barbara. He had seen them out together a couple of times. He chalked it off because Chad seemed genuine in his love for Katrina, but maybe Chad wasn't as great a man as Bo had thought. On the other hand, Barbara was a beautiful woman, and who could blame Chad for not taking what's being offered on a silver platter? Bo smiled to himself.

This whole thing was getting out of hand. He had no idea where it was going to end, if it hadn't already.

CHAPTER ELEVEN

At first, Chad was annoyed when Barbara approached him. He just wanted to be left alone. All women were trouble. He should have remembered that from his first marriage. He had sworn to never fall in love again. "Stupid fool," he chided himself.

"Chad, where ye off to? The evening's still young." Barbara wrapped her arms around Chad's left arm as she walked next to him.

"I am really not in the mood to party anymore, Barbara. Do not let me pull you away. You go on back and have fun. I am going to turn in early."

"Nonsense, Chad. I'll be going back with ye. I have to admit these new shoes I bought are killing me toes. I sure am glad it's not too far to home. I might have been askin' ye to carry me."

Chad knew she was just being friendly, but he didn't want a friendly woman around right now. He also didn't want to be rude, so he let her chatter all the way home, all the while hanging on his left arm as if they were lovers.

Chad thought they would never reach the house and was glad to see it when they turned the corner.

"Would ye be liken a nightcap, Chad?" Barbara's voice was husky. Chad had no doubt what she had on her mind and what she was offering, and if things were different, he just might have taken her up on her offer. But they weren't.

"Barbara, I am still a married man, and until she gives me the document showing me different, I am going to have to honor those vows. I appreciate all that you have done for me, though. Thanks for walking home with me, but I am going to turn in now."

Barbara was very disappointed when Chad walked up the stairs and closed his bedroom door.

"Damn, this is going to be harder than I thought. He would make me a perfect husband. I will just have to prove to him I will make him the perfect wife." But how? She didn't know.

The following morning, Katrina saddled her horse. She wasn't going to wait another minute to get this annulment over with. She had been awake all night long just waiting for the sun to rise. She wanted this whole thing to end. She couldn't wait to slap those papers in Chad's hands.

Chad had gone to have breakfast early. He wanted out of Barbara's place before she got up. Luckily it was Sunday, and she didn't make a big breakfast for all her boarders. She went to church, so she slept in, and they could fix whatever they wanted. It was her day of rest.

When Chad came out of the diner, he saw Katrina knocking on the judge's office door. The little fool was going to go through with it. Well, he intended to have a few words with her first.

Chad walked across the street with a purpose—the purpose to put some sense into her pretty little head.

Katrina was looking into the window of the office. It was dark inside. Surely, they weren't closed because it was Sunday. People still needed legal advice on Sundays, didn't they? Katrina jumped with a start when she heard Chad's voice.

"They are closed on Sundays, Katrina. You will just have to be married to me for one more day." The sarcasm was evident in his tone.

"Oh, Chad, you scared me." She put her hand over her heart and looked down. "I was hoping to get this ordeal over with." Her voice was shaking. She had really hoped to not run into Chad today.

They both stared at each other in silence. Katrina wanted to fall apart, but she wouldn't. She kept reminding herself she was stronger than that.

"I should have made love to you when I had the opportunity," Chad declared softly. Katrina was stunned by his words.

"Chad!" she tried to scold. "Why on earth would you say such a thing?" Katrina felt very warm all over.

"Because if I had made love to you, then you would not be able to annul this marriage. We would have consummated this marriage, and instead of me sleeping alone again, I would have you next to me."

Chad watched as many things went through her mind. Her facial expressions changed rapidly.

Katrina was elated to hear he was sleeping alone. She was excited to know he wanted her to be sleeping next to him. Her stomach had butterflies in it just thinking of the love they could have shared. She wanted to be married to Chad more than anything, but she wanted him to ask her, of his own free will, not those of a tribe leader.

"Look at me, Trina," Chad asked her quietly as he gently cupped her chin and lifted her head to have eye contact.

Katrina looked up, and as soon as their eyes met, he pulled her into his arms and kissed her with all the hunger he had been keeping walled up inside.

At first, Katrina was alarmed with worry of what people would think of Chad kissing her outside for the whole world to see. Those fears didn't last long. Chad was kissing her and holding her so tight she couldn't think straight anymore. Katrina gave into the kiss, and Chad knew exactly when she gave up the fight. Katrina wrapped her fingers in his hair, and if possible, she pulled him even closer.

Chad moaned deep in his throat. "Trina, you are killing me. I have to have you."

"Chad, you cannot."

"Why not?"

"What would people think?"

"I do not give a damn what people think. You are my wife. I want you more than anything I have ever wanted. You have been driving me crazy. I want to finalize this whole thing. I want to find the minister and repeat my vows to you. As a matter of fact, everyone will be at church this morning, including your ma and brothers." Chad grabbed her hand and started pulling her down the street. "Let's go get remarried so that I can make you my real wife." Chad held his breath. He had been pulling her along as he was headed for the church, and Katrina stopped dead in her tracks, yanking her hand out of his.

"Chad, what are you saying? Stop! I want you to do this right."

Chad looked at Katrina. She was so beautiful. She had on the riding outfit that she and her ma had made. It was pretty but probably not something she would want to be married in. He had to ask anyway.

"Trina, wait." Chad looked around. They were only a half block from the church, and everyone was arriving. Chad got down on one knee.

"Trina, I want more than anything for you to be my wife. I am so in love with you. I have been miserable without you sleeping next to me. I got used to holding you each night, and now I feel empty without you beside me all the time. Please, will you marry me? Today? In that church?" Chad pointed. "In front of these townsfolk?" They both looked around and saw everyone staring.

Katrina had just got the proposal that she had been praying for. Her eyes filled with tears.

Chad's heart stopped. If she said no, life would be over for him.

Katrina got down on her knees in front of Chad and looked into his eyes. "Chad, I have been in love with you from the moment you stepped foot onto our ranch. My heart was broken last night when you left the dance. I looked all over for you to dance with, and when I saw you left with Barbara, I thought I would die. I won't be marrying a man who is a cheatin' scoundrel, though. You have to give up your relationship with her before I will say yes."

Chad's face broke out into a big smile. "Trina darlin', there has been no affair goin' on with Barbara or any other woman for that matter. You have been the only woman this mind and body of mine would allow in. I want you as my wife, and if you will say yes, I promise you I will do everything in my power to prove to you each and every day how much I love you."

Chad and Katrina had no idea of how many more of the townsfolk had shown up, including her family and Barbara, waiting for her answer. They had tuned everyone and everything out.

"Yes, Chad, I will be your wife."

The roar of applause was deafening. Chad and Katrina stood up instantly. Katrina was so embarrassed, and Chad was overly elated. He picked Katrina up and twirled her around.

"Seal it with a kiss, Katrina," Chad challenged her to kiss him in front of everyone.

Katrina looked over and saw Bo wink at her. She was being held up in the air by Chad, holding onto his shoulders. Then she bent and wrapped her arms around his neck and sealed the proposal with a kiss that the entire town cheered on. Barbara just shook her head in disbelief, saddened by lost hope.

If Katrina had thought Chad had kissed her to the point of curling her toes as much as possible, she had been completely wrong. This kiss was like no other. The intimacy of this kiss made her whole body burn all the way to her inner core.

When Chad pulled away, Katrina was breathless.

"*Wow,*" she said as she laid her forehead against his with shaky knees.

"*Wow* is right," Chad echoed, bewildered by the impact of their kiss. Then Chad slid Katrina down his body and chuckled when she looked up with surprise in her eyes as she felt his arousal.

"Chad!" she squeaked out.

"Yes, my little Trina," Chad whispered. "You do that to me. I am afraid I am going to have to keep you close for a minute or two, or I am going to embarrass the both of us in front of our townsfolk." Chad noticed most of them had started to enter the church.

Katrina turned every shade of red, which caused Chad to laugh the most heartwarming laugh. He gave her a big hug. He just couldn't get enough of her.

"I know you are not dressed for a wedding, Trina, but I need you to be my wife today." Chad pulled her up against his arousal to emphasize his need.

"Chad, are you saying you want to get married right now?"

"I am, Trina. As far as I am concerned, the words I spoke in the Indian camp were real, but obviously you did not think so, so I want for your benefit to repeat them. I cannot wait another day. I want you next to me always. I need to hold you in my arms. I need you to be really mine."

His words were so warming, and although she had never been one for all the frills, she had dreamed of a planned wedding: a wedding dress, flowers, a cake, etc. She looked at her riding outfit and cringed. "Chad, you want me to be married looking like this?" She couldn't help but feel a little disappointed.

Chad could see her reluctance. He could see she needed a real wedding, a little more planning. After all, that was the thing most little girls dreamed of and looked forward to—their wedding day.

"How about we get married at dusk? That way, you can be a little more prepared. We can go into the church and invite all to attend. But I will not spend another night without you, Trina."

Katrina knew she had her mother's wedding dress to wear. Her mother could make a few quick alterations to it, and the flowers would be no problem.

Chad went on. "We could throw a reception next Saturday at the ranch after we have had a week's honeymoon. What do you say, Trina?"

Chad watched as Katrina walked down the aisle on Bo's arm. What a vision she made in her mother's wedding gown. His heart swelled with pride. For a brief second, he had remembered he would never do this again, but just for a brief second because marrying Katrina felt so right.

As Katrina stopped in front of Chad and faced him, she began to shake uncontrollably. Chad took both her hands in his and squeezed them.

They looked into each other's eyes, and Chad quietly asked, "Okay?"

Katrina nodded and smiled. God, how she loved this man.

"Who gives this woman in marriage?" the town minister asked.

"Her ma and I," Bo proudly stated then sat by his ma and held her hand.

The ceremony went quick. "You may now kiss your bride," Chad was told by the minister.

Chad lifted Katrina's veil. He cupped her face with both hands and looked deep into her eyes. "I love you, Mrs. Miles." Then he devoured her mouth. Everyone was encouraging his bold kiss.

Katrina was pleasantly surprised. She loved the sound of her new name, but more than that, she loved the way Chad could knock her boots off with his kisses. If his kiss this afternoon could be so different than the others and then this kiss could be more potent than this afternoon's, what would tonight's kisses be like? She shivered just thinking about it. For the oddest reason, she didn't understand. She wasn't scared. She totally trusted Chad.

Chad turned to all their friends. "I hope you will all join us out at the Holt ranch next Saturday for our reception. It will start at the noon meal."

The congregation clapped with their approval, and Chad took Katrina's hand and headed down the aisle. Everyone gathered outside as Chad lifted Katrina onto his horse. He set her sidesaddle and mounted behind her. Their friends tossed rice at them as they rode away.

"Where are we going, Chad?" Katrina hadn't given much thought to where they would go for a honeymoon.

"Oh, I have just the spot for us." Chad headed Streak toward the hills.

As they rode, Chad kept kissing her. His hands were all over her. "I do not think I am going to be able to wait to have you, Katrina."

Everywhere Chad touched her, she was on fire. The anticipation was driving them both crazy with need. When he ended that kiss, Katrina sighed, "How much longer?"

"Soon," Chad answered in pain.

One hour after they left town, they reached a campsite that had been set up.

Katrina was amazed. "Chad, you thought of everything except I think we are going to freeze to death."

"I felt this atmosphere is what made me fall in love with you, so I wanted to make love to you for the first time out under the stars. As for freezing, remember what I said about two naked bodies?"

Katrina blushed as Chad wrapped her in his arms.

"I promise I will not let you freeze, my little Trina." Then Chad kissed her with all the hunger he had been feeling for weeks. The kiss was playful at first with him nibbling her bottom lip, then he sucked on her lip then her tongue as he deepened the kiss. Katrina became very warm all over, confirming that there was no way she would ever get cold next to Chad.

Katrina was out of breath when Chad pulled away. *"Double wow,"* she panted.

"Double wow is right!" Chad echoed.

A couple hours later, Chad asked his real wife, "Are you okay?" Once they had gotten off Streak, Chad lost all control. He was pleasantly surprised to see Katrina do the same. They were both out of their clothes in record time and in each other's arms within minutes. The lovemaking had started out quick and frantic, but Chad fortunately came to his senses before entering her as a virgin because he could have hurt her if he hadn't stopped to think.

"I could not be better." She smiled at him. "That was more than I could have ever dreamed of." She looked down and then up into his eyes with an embarrassed expression. "Could we do that again?"

Be still my heart, he thought. *I have married myself a little nymph.* "Well, I have got news for you, sugar. It will only keep getting better with experience." Chad gave her a big hug. "And as long as you do not get too sore, we can do that all night."

"Did I disappoint you?" Suddenly Katrina felt self-conscious.

"No way, you did not disappoint me. I was the one out of control. Let me show you how a tender lover can be, not some out-of-control, need-you-now, right-this-minute, deprived lover is." Chad was making all kinds of crazy faces at Katrina, one to match each description of the different lovers he just described to her. Katrina was laughing hysterically at him. They were both laughing out of control. It felt good to be so comfortable with him now.

Chad got up and lifted his hands to the heavens and yelled at the top of his lungs, "I love my little Trina. I love my little Trina." He was stark naked and in love.

Katrina got up and went to him with so much love in her heart. Then she whispered in his ear, "I love you more."

Chad wrapped his arms around her and held her so tight. "I feel so blessed to have you for my wife, and I promise I will do everything I can to make you happy forever, Trina. Just always keep loving me, okay?"

"Chad, you forget I have loved you for four years already. I could never stop loving you. I promise you that." She looked into his eyes filled with so much love she could read it. "You are just a slow learner," she teased.

"Not anymore. I plan to be the teacher. Come back to our bed, and I will teach you some more tonight." He wiggled his eyebrows at her.

"You are on, cowboy. Teach me all you know. I am a quick learner."

A couple hours later, Chad smiled down at her. "What are you thinking right now?" she asked.

"I do not think. I know that you are a quick learner. And you are so beautiful when you blush that way." It was already dawn. They hadn't slept a wink, and with the sunrise, her pretty complexion was bright pink from his compliment. All Chad could do was wonder how he had gotten so lucky.

"Chad, have you given it any thought on where we are going to live?"

"Well, I have but do not have an answer right now. Why, do you have a suggestion?"

"Well, it was my daddy's dream that all of us would settle on the ranch. We each have a portion of land, and I was hoping we could build something close to Mama."

"I would love to do that. I really did not want to go too far away. How about we get cleaned up and head on over to the ranch, and you could show me what you had in mind."

CHAPTER TWELVE

It didn't take long for them to pack up and ride out to the ranch. They were met by those that weren't out on the range with congratulations. Everyone seemed genuinely happy for the new couple. Evelyn asked them to come into the kitchen. She had something she wanted to discuss with them.

Bo joined them at the table for a cup of coffee. He started the conversation, "Chad, Katrina, Ma and I thought the two of you could take over the main house, and we could put up a smaller place for Ma next door." Both Katrina and Chad started to protest that they didn't want to run Ma out of her house.

Evelyn put up her hands to stop everyone from talking at the same time. "Look, this place has gotten too big for me to keep up. We could build a four-bedroom place next door, and the boys could move out with me, and in the meantime, you two could start filling up the six bedrooms of this house with your own little ones."

"Mama." This made Katrina blush.

"I like your ma's suggestions of a bunch of little ones," Chad chimed in. "And practice makes perfect," he added just to see her turn completely red, wiggling his eyebrows at her. Everyone just laughed together.

"Chad!" Katrina smacked his knee out of embarrassment.

Evelyn continued, "I know it will take time to build a new place, so, Katrina, I hope you do not mind, but I took the liberty of having your brothers help me move my belongings out of the master bedroom and move all of yours and Chad's belongings in."

"Mama, I do not know what to say." Katrina felt overwhelmed.

"Say you two will stay here with us. I do not want you to leave. I need you here close by."

Katrina got up and hugged her ma. "I did not have any intentions of going away again, Mama. I need you too. We will be happy to stay. Right, Chad?"

"Yes, ma'am, we will." Chad winked at Katrina. He loved this whole family, even those little hoodlums, Tim and Tom, who had become quite scarce lately. Along with James, you couldn't help but wonder what they had been up to lately.

That evening, when Katrina and Chad went to climb into their bed in her parents' old bedroom, they came across one of the boys' pranks. Chad went to crawl into bed first, but his feet came up short. He couldn't stretch his legs out. He didn't say anything to Katrina and had a hard time keeping a straight face sitting on the side of the bed until she went to climb in between the sheets.

They both looked at each other and burst out laughing. The boys hadn't played any pranks on Katrina since the watering hole, and she felt a little disappointed, thinking that they were going to stop and take the excitement out of sibling rivalry. She was glad that the war was back on. She and Chad worked together to put the sheets on right, plotting out their revenge.

As Katrina lay in his arms, she sighed, "Ya know I have never had anyone to plot with me before. It has always been them against me. This is fun having a coheart, someone on my team for a change to help me out. What do you suggest?"

"I suggest you give me a kiss for now. I have other things on my mind." He proved to her he meant every word when he pulled her up against his arousal.

"I knew I married a smart man. I just knew it." She giggled as he nudged her neck. "I love you, Chad Miles."

"I love you more, Katrina Miles," he whispered in her ear.

Katrina loved the sound of her new name on his lips. And oh, those lips knew just how to please her. Chad was devouring her with his mouth, and her whole body felt on fire. His hands knew just how to put her under his spell. She fell asleep with a smile on her lips.

Several months flew by in a flash. Every hand, when not out on the ranch, put in extra time helping Bo and Chad on the new house. Digging the hole for a good-sized cellar was the biggest part of the job, and now the foundation was secure on top of the cellar and the material was cut for the exterior walls.

This weekend, they were hosting a house-raising party with all the surrounding farms joining them to raise the walls. Katrina and Evelyn had been in the kitchen for days, preparing meals to feed everyone a hearty lunch and supper. There just seemed to be so much good energy for the family, and Katrina was on cloud nine with the love and tenderness she and Chad felt for each other.

Evelyn looked over at her daughter, who was smiling as she took another batch of cookies out of the oven, and felt Katrina never looked more beautiful.

"If I did not know better, Katrina, I would say you have a glow about you." Katrina's head came up quickly to look at her ma.

"What on earth do you mean, Mama?" she asked, confused.

"Just that you seem very happy with Chad. I knew he would be a good man for you."

"Oh, he is, Mama. He is always doin' somethin' to make me feel special. Daddy would have been very pleased with Chad."

Evelyn just nodded her head in agreement. Evelyn knew it, but Katrina didn't. Katrina was with child already, and Evelyn didn't want to spoil the surprise for her figuring it out on her own. Oh, she would drop a hint here and there, but she wanted this lesson to be on Katrina. There had been several signs that Evelyn knew to be early pregnancy signals: a little morning nausea that Katrina kept shaking off, the increase in her appetite, getting tired earlier in the evening, a couple times of nausea when Evelyn was cooking, but the most recent telltale sign was the baby bump that Katrina hadn't paid much attention to.

Her little tomboy was turning into quite the little housewife. Oh, she still spent plenty of time outdoors, taking care of the ranch with Chad and Bo, but she spent a majority inside with Evelyn, preparing special meals for Chad and all the other men on the property. It was nice, the two of them working together. Evelyn never minded doing all the household chores alone before, but as she got older, it was much nicer having a companion.

Katrina heard the first of the neighbors coming into the yard, so she ran to the door to greet them. Out on the porch, she saw a whole wagonload of men from town. "Mornin', Ms. Katrina, Evelyn." William took off his hat and nodded at the two of them on the steps. "Hope you do not mind, but a few of the men wanted to help out today."

Katrina giggled and looked over at her ma with such surprise and gratitude. To William and the men, she said, "Not at all. The more, the merrier." To her ma, she said, "Better be gettin' some more vittles together for this wonderful surprise."

Evelyn nodded in agreement and responded to William, "Thank you, William. We appreciate all the help we can get. Gentlemen, thank you in advance. Lunch will be served in three hours and supper at six. You will find Bo and Chad around the corner of the house gettin' started."

William smacked the reins on the horses' rumps and headed around the corner with the wagon, and Katrina and Evelyn went back inside.

"Katrina, I am goin' to put a large pot of potatoes on to boil for potato salad. Will you quick soak some beans, and we will get a pan of baked beans going for the supper meal? That ought to stretch enough for the extra people." Katrina nodded in agreement, and they both got to work.

A few minutes later, they heard another wagon pulling into the yard then another before they even got to the door. This time, it was the Johnsons and the Boyers, two of the surrounding families, with the women and children too. Both women were helped down from the wagons by their husbands. "Wonderful to see you both." Evelyn was smiling.

Mr. Johnson walked around to the back of the wagon. "Where would you like me to put these dishes?" he asked Katrina.

"Oh, let me help you with those," Katrina responded as she took two of the pie plates.

"You did not have to do that," Evelyn gratefully praised.

"It was my pleasure, Evelyn. I do not think you know how big this house-raisin party is goin' to get. I heard talk in town yesterday that everyone around is plannin' on joinin' in on this fun," Mrs. Johnson informed her.

"Yes," Mrs. Boyer agreed. "I also brought several dishes, and a few of the other wives are doing the same. This is goin' to be one big shin dig."

"Well, I guess I never expected this much attention from the town folk, but why not?" Evelyn beamed, and they all laughed together.

Katrina walked around the house to the construction site. She felt overwhelmed with all the friends that were there to help erect the house.

Tears were welling up in her eyes. She wiped away one that slipped down her cheek.

Chad was giving instructions to several of the men on how they were going to pull the walls up with the aid of horses. Everyone was in agreement on how this house was going to be put together. He looked up and saw Trina off to the side wiping away tears. "Be right back, men," he said as he walked over to his beautiful wife.

"Everything okay?" Chad asked Katrina as he wiped another tear from her chin.

"Yes! Just feeling emotional I guess." Katrina looked into his concerned eyes. Chad kissed her forehead and pulled her into a hug.

After a couple of seconds, he set her away from him and said, "Mrs. Miles, I got work to do, and if I hold you much longer, I will be having to excuse myself."

Katrina's eyes got very wide. "Chad, hush yourself. Someone will hear you," she scolded.

Chad chuckled at her then turned her toward the house and smacked her rump. "Go help your ma. I got this end of things covered."

Katrina headed in that direction but stopped and turned to watch him for a few more minutes. "How did I get so lucky?" she asked herself.

Back around the front of the house, several more families had arrived, and as Mrs. Boyer said, they were all bringing dishes to feed the hungry workers. This was going to be a wonderful day on the Holt Ranch.

At noon, the women had all the tables set up, laden with every kind of dish you could think of. They had set up under two large old oaks. Katrina walked around the side of the house to chime the dinner bell and was shocked at what she saw. In just a few hours, all the exterior walls were up.

Before she rang the bell, she went back to call for her ma to come and see the progress. The two of them stood there in awe of how fast the house was coming together.

Bo walked up to them. "Well, Ma, what do you think?"

"Bo, how on earth did this happen so fast?" she was exasperated.

"Well, I wish I could take the credit, but it was Chad. He marked everything out on where it was to match, like a puzzle, and we just all put it together and stood it up. At this rate, we will have this house done in two weeks." Bo beamed at them. "Chad is a genius."

Katrina swelled with pride over the man she married. "Where is my husband anyway?" She looked around for him but didn't see him.

"He is around here somewhere." Bo took the bell from his ma and rang it. "I am starvin'. Can we eat now?"

"Of course, of course." Evelyn walked back to the front of the house with Bo.

Katrina went to find Chad. He was inside, checking a few things over. She walked up behind him and wrapped her arms around his waist from behind.

"You better not let my wife catch you. She might scratch your eyes out." He laughed as he turned in her arms and kissed her.

"I would too, you know? Did I ever tell you I think you are wonderful?" She beamed at him.

Chad kissed her again and pulled her up against him. "I cannot wait to have you tonight."

Katrina just shook her head at him. "Do you ever think of anything other than that Mr. Miles?"

"Not when I have you in my arms." He squeezed her tighter.

"Ahem." James cleared his throat. "You two think you can break that up long enough to grace our lunch, Chad?"

Chad groaned, "Be right there, James." Then he turned to Katrina. "See what kind of trouble you get me into?" He smiled at her.

"Me?" she questioned as Chad took her hand and headed to the front of the main house.

As they all sat and ate lunch, Katrina looked around at the familiar faces and some not so familiar. She was asking Chad if he knew everyone there, and he had to admit there were a couple he didn't know.

"Some new folk in town, I guess. Awful nice of them to want to pitch in," he continued. "After we eat, I will introduce myself to them to make sure they know I appreciate their help."

Katrina looked over at him. "Ya know, all the kitchen duties are bein' handled pretty well. Could I help some?" She was itching to get outside, he could tell.

"Sure!" One simple word was all it took from him to put a huge smile on her face. He loved her smile.

"I will go change and meet you out back." Katrina hopped up and then almost toppled over.

"Whoa there." Chad grabbed her. "You okay?"

"I guess I stood up too fast. I am okay now."

"Are you sure? You look a little pale." His concern was evident.

"I am fine really. I just got up really fast from being excited. I am going to change now. Will you let Ma know that I am going to help you?"

"Sure," he pretty much said to himself since she was already gone.

Chad walked over to Evelyn to let her know Katrina was wanting to help with the house and was a little surprised with her question.

"Do you really think that is a good idea, Chad?"

"I do not see any reason why unless you need her to help in the kitchen, but if that is the case you get to tell her."

Evelyn decided to keep her suspicions to herself. It was obvious Chad had no idea of Katrina's condition. She knew Chad would keep a close eye on her, but she needed to at least ask it of him.

"Just watch over her, Chad. There are a lot of workers that might not be as careful of her as you would. Keep her close."

"Of course. Is there something I need to know, Evelyn?" Chad stared her in the eyes.

"No, no, I just do not want to see her get hurt is all."

Chad wasn't buying it, but he would do as she asked without even being asked because that was his job as her husband, to keep her safe. He walked away feeling odd, like he was missing something.

Katrina was in her bedroom trying to find a pair of pants that would fit. "Ohhhh, this is so frustrating," she was berating herself. "This is what you get for eating like such a pig since you got married, missy." She just could not believe that she could not button or zip any of her pants. Chad's pants would be way too big on her, so would Bo's. Katrina went into Tim and Tom's room and found a pair of pants in there, and sure enough, they fit but were way too long, so she just rolled them up.

"You young lady are going on a diet starting this week." Katrina told herself in the mirror. Satisfied she found something to wear, she headed out to the building site.

Katrina walked up to Chad. "I am ready. What do you want me to do?"

Chad looked her up and down. "Are you okay? Is there something wrong?" Something about her seemed out of place.

Katrina looked down at herself. "I do not think so." She looked back up at Chad. "I knew it. You can tell I am gettin' fat." She almost cried.

Chad never thought any such thing, so he had no clue where that was coming from. "What?"

Katrina stomped off madder than a wet hen at him. It looked like they were having their first fight since they got married, and he wasn't even sure why. Chad heard his name being called "Ahhh, hell!" He turned back to the job to be done. He would have to deal with her later.

Evelyn saw Katrina heading into the house, and she looked to be very upset, so she excused herself from the group of ladies she was talking to. She found Katrina in her room, crying.

"What is it? Did you get hurt?" Evelyn sat next to her on the bed.

Katrina sat up and wiped her eyes. "Mama, I am getting so fat. None of my pants fit me, and Chad noticed it too."

Evelyn looked at her with such love. "You are not getting fat, dear."

"I am," Katrina cried again.

Katrina was so upset Evelyn decided she needed to do a little more than hint now. "Let me ask you a question. When was the last time you had your monthly?"

"What does that have to do with anythin', Ma?" Katrina looked confused at first, then her eyes got really wide. She had been having such a wonderful time lately she hadn't even noticed she had missed her monthly. She thought about it for a minute then her eyes got even wider. "Mama, I have not had my monthly since Chad and I got married."

"As I thought," Evelyn said matter-of-factly. "That would make you four months."

Evelyn didn't think Katrina's eyes could get any wider, but they sure did. Evelyn laughed out loud as the realization hit Katrina. "Four months? Oh my gosh. That explains everything now. I am not fat. I am with child." Katrina's hands went to her tummy as she looked down in awe then back up at her mother. "Oh, Mama, this is wonderful news. I need to tell Chad right away." Katrina gave her mother a big hug then went to run out of the room but stopped at the door and asked, "How did you know, Ma?"

"Oh, there were little signs here and there, but now look at your little bump." Evelyn went to her daughter and put her hand on her tummy. "I cannot wait to be a grandma," Evelyn whispered.

Katrina hugged her again. "I love you, Mama." Then excitedly ran out of the house. A baby! She and Chad were going to have a baby.

Katrina found Chad, but he was really busy giving orders, so she decided to wait till later to share their wonderful news. She looked down at herself and decided to go put on one of her prettier dresses. She wanted to be as pretty as she could for Chad when she told him.

An hour later, Katrina walked out onto the porch in a beautiful gown that she and her mother had worked on. The sweetheart neckline emphasized how full her breast had gotten. It was almost too tight. She did have a little baby bump, but only those that knew she was with child would recognize it to be so. The most striking was her beautiful hair. Katrina rarely wore it down and loose. Even when she went to bed, she kept it braided so she and Chad wouldn't get tangled up in it.

It seemed as if everyone was drawn to her beauty because it got quiet all of a sudden as all eyes turned to her. Katrina felt very self-conscious all of a sudden and turned to go back in the house when Chad called out to her, "Trina."

Chad had walked around the corner of the house just as Katrina had stepped out onto the porch. He stopped dead in his tracks along with the others. They were calling it a day. Katrina stood there, looking more beautiful than he could ever remember. Something was different about her. He knew she dolled herself up, and her hair was breathtaking, but there was something else that he just couldn't put his finger on. As she turned, he heard one of the men make a comment.

"You better guard that beauty, Chad. She keeps it hidden really well."

Several of the others agreed, and Chad felt a stab of jealousy. Katrina looked like she was retreating, so he called out to her. He didn't want her to disappear on him. He thought he might owe her an apology. She was very mad at him the last time he saw her.

Katrina turned to his voice with a radiant smile on her face. They headed toward each other, paying no attention to all the eyes that were on them.

"Sorry," they said in unison and laughed together as Chad took her in his arms.

When he pulled away and looked down at her, she had tears pooled in her eyes. "What is it, Trina? You seem to be so emotional lately. I do not even know how I made you angry earlier. By the way, you look angelic right now. Do you know that?" Chad wiped the tear that escaped down her cheek away with his thumb.

Katrina put her hands on both sides of his face. "I need to talk to you."

Just as Chad was to respond, two little boys ran right into them, jolting them apart. "Damn kids," Chad ground out.

Katrina was alarmed to hear the anger in his voice. Maybe she was assuming he would be happy about the baby. Maybe he didn't like kids at all. They really hadn't talked too much about a family. They were just newly married and all. Maybe this wasn't the time to tell him after all.

Chad could see the change in Katrina right away. Her joy was ruined by the boys, and he wanted to see her beautiful smile again. "Are you okay? Did they hurt you?" Katrina was distracted. "Trina, what did you want to talk about? Do not let those heathens ruin your mood."

Heathens! Who calls children heathens? Did she marry a monster? Katrina felt like she didn't know Chad at all. "No! I am fine. Chad, we will talk later. I need to help Mama right now." She turned to walk away, so Chad grabbed her hand to stall her. "Chad, please, later," she sounded desperate to get away from him, and he didn't want to make a scene, so he let her go.

Katrina almost ran away from him. Chad was so frustrated that he couldn't seem to do anything right in the last couple of days. What was the matter with her?

Katrina was afraid she was going to fall apart. Chad didn't like kids after all. What was she going to do? Right now she needed to keep herself busy. She couldn't think about this right now. Taking over for her ma, who looked like she was going to drop any second now, would keep her mind busy. "Mama, I'll serve. Please get yourself a plate and rest awhile."

Evelyn kissed Katrina's cheek. "Thank you. I am a bit exhausted."

Katrina put on the best smile she could. Chad could see it wasn't reaching her eyes anymore, but anybody that didn't know her as well as he did wouldn't be able to tell she was bothered by something. As he went through the line and got a plate full of scrumptious dishes, he was watching her every move. By all pretenses, she looked happy and beautiful. Chad watched as each single man that was served by her beamed with gratitude. He hated it when he felt jealous. They were married now. She was his, and he knew none of these men would overstep that boundary.

Chad stood in front of Katrina, and her smile went away. What in the world had he done to have her looking so sad all of a sudden? He didn't want to make a scene, but he had the notion to just grab her hand and take her to their bedroom and get her to spill her guts out to him. This was driving him crazy.

Katrina gave Chad a huge spoonful of beans. They had eye contact, and her stomach lurched. She caught herself just before she put her hand on her abdomen. She found it amazing how she wanted to protect her child just out of reflex. Would Chad hate their baby? Katrina pretty much dismissed him by turning to Charles, the next person in line.

Chad took the hint and went onto the next dish. He was determined to have this out tonight, though.

Hours later, the last of the crowd left. Katrina was still in the kitchen, putting the last of the desserts away. She knew she would only be starting this again tomorrow but with fewer people. Most of the men folk were coming back and just a few of the women folk. The progress was remarkable. Katrina couldn't be more grateful for all the help but mostly for Chad. She had shied away from him as much as possible the rest of the evening, but now she needed to get some shut-eye, and she knew he would want to talk. Chad hadn't come in from the yard yet, so she rushed off to get ready for bed. If she were lucky, she could be asleep before he came to bed.

Chad sat out by the barn. He could see Katrina through the door, wiping her hands and then heading to their bedroom. He was hurt at how she avoided him all evening. She would be all smiles for everyone else, but as soon as they would have eye contact, she would look away immediately. He just didn't get it. What had he done?

Well, there was only one way to find out. He shoved himself out of the chair and stretched. His body ached all over. Tomorrow was going to be hell. He sure hoped tonight wasn't.

Katrina already lay in bed when he got to their bedroom. She was in a cotton gown that covered her from head to toe. She hadn't slept in anything since they said their vows, so this was a telltale sign that she wasn't planning on making love to him tonight. Damn, he was frustrated.

Chad stripped off his clothes and climbed in behind Katrina. He pulled her up against him and nuzzled her neck. He had no clue what he had done to upset her, but he wanted to set it right before they went to sleep.

"Trina, can we talk please?"

Chad whispering in her ear sent a chill up and down her spine. Oh, how she loved this man, but if he didn't want children, there was going to be a problem.

Katrina rolled over in his arms to face him. Chad could tell she had been crying again. He just shook his head in dismay. "What the hell have I done to make you cry so much lately? I swear I have no idea."

Katrina just fell apart and started crying harder. Chad pulled her in closer and waited for the sobs to subside. He rubbed her back and spoke softly to her. As he was consoling her, it dawned on her that he wasn't a monster after all. A monster wouldn't be so gentle.

Katrina pulled away from him just enough to talk, but her words were muffled against his chest, so Chad pushed away a little more. "I am sorry I could not understand you."

"Chad, I am just going to say it, and if you are mad, I am sorry. I never expected this to happen so fast." She paused to gather some courage. Chad waited patiently. He was afraid if he interrupted her, she would start to cry again.

"I am with child." Katrina ducked her head really fast. She didn't want to see his anger. If she had been looking, she would have seen him go from shocked to sheer joy.

Chad cupped her chin to look up at him. "Why on earth would you think I would be mad? Please stop crying. I cannot take the tears anymore."

"Because you do not like children," she cried even harder.

"Where on earth did you get that idea, silly woman? I like kids." Chad couldn't believe it. He was going to be a daddy. Yes, it was quick. Quicker than he could have hoped for, but he was overjoyed by her news.

"You called the boys heathens. That's a horrible name for children."

Chad burst out with laughter. "That is what their daddy calls them in an endearing way. I do not even know their names, so I just repeated what I knew. All this worry cannot be good for our baby. Do you hear me? No more worries. Our baby will be loved and cherished as much as I love and cherish their mama. Now come here and let me show you how much I cherish your body and take this ugly thing off." Chad was grabbing the night dress she was wearing. "Promise me you will never wear anything like this again, not even when you are in your old age."

His smile and wicked look on his face told her all she needed to know about this wonderful man she had fallen in love with.

Chad pulled the night dress the rest of the way off and put his hand over her barely protruding tummy. There was definitely a baby growing in there. Everything made perfect sense to him now. The mood swings, crying all the time, little dizzy spells, and the larger appetite. His woman was quite a woman, and he was so proud to be her man.

CHAPTER THIRTEEN

The following month flew by. The new house had been completely erected. Evelyn, Bo, Tim, and Tom had moved out of the big house, and everyone was settled into their new rooms.

Katrina and Chad continued to have the main meals in the main house, and Evelyn and Katrina fell into a nice routine of keeping both homes in perfect order.

Katrina couldn't believe how quickly her baby was growing. She and her mama had to do some quick sewing for some new clothes for her big belly. Her dresses were way too tight across the bodice. Her breast, which Chad seemed to be overjoyed about, were huge already, and she hadn't even gotten any milk in them.

Katrina was trying on one of the dresses she and her ma had started last week, and something just wasn't right. "Mama, what is going on here? It cannot be too small. We just measured me."

Evelyn got up to zip the back up, and sure enough, it was not going to zip. She was worried this could be the case for Katrina. She really hoped Chad and her could have a couple of children before twins came into the picture like it had for her. Bo and Katrina were her first set of twins, then James, and then the second set of twins, Tim and Tom. Tim and Tom were easy because she had the other children to help out, but twins, to begin with, was torture.

"Ewww, Mama, this is so frustrating. If this one is too small already, that means the others are going to be too small also. We should just make me some sacks. Poke a hole at the top for my head and two on the sides for arms, if this is how it is going to be." Katrina just wanted to cry.

"Now you look here, missy," Evelyn scolded. "You will get up and put something pretty on every day no matter how awful and fat you might think you feel. This way, you feel better about yourself. Now sit down. I need to tell you something that might hit you a little hard."

"What? Do you think there is something wrong?" Katrina's worry was evident.

"No, nothing wrong, but I have a suspicion, and you know I usually am right about these things." Evelyn hesitated, not sure how Katrina was going to react.

"What is it, Mama? What do you need to tell me?"

"I think you are carrying twins." Evelyn burst out and giggled.

Katrina went white. Twins? Well, she was a twin. Why wouldn't she have put that together herself? It just hadn't dawned on her that she would be carrying more than one baby. "Oh my word, Mama. What are the signs of twins instead of just one baby?"

"Well, in a lot of ways, everything is the same except in some ways. There are other signs to look for, and because I have had two sets of twins, I know what to look for. For example, your belly is way larger than most women who are five months along. Your breast have doubled in size without your milk even coming in yet. Not to mention you are a twin, and twins run in the family."

Just then Katrina felt movement for the first time. "Oh!" she said in awe.

"What is it?" Evelyn asked

Katrina took her mama's hand and put it on her belly. "I felt the baby or babies move."

Evelyn felt for a couple seconds then said. "You will probably feel a lot more before anyone can feel it from the outside. You should go find Chad and share your news with him."

"How do you think he will react, Mama?" Twins, not one but two babies. It just seemed life got better and better, or was it scarier and scarier? Katrina wasn't sure anymore.

"Oh, I think he will be just fine. Chad seems to go along with whatever is thrown at him. He always has." Evelyn had always felt a security in Chad being part of the Holt Ranch family even before he was really family. "Go find your husband."

Katrina stood up, and they both realized her dress wasn't zipped and laughed in unison. "First, I need to find something to wear." They laughed even louder with joy.

Katrina found Chad out behind the barn, oiling down a group of saddles. Before she interrupted him, she just stood and watched him work. He was so handsome. She wondered what their children would look like. Would they look just like their daddy? Would they be boys or girls or both?

Chad had been in such a great mood. He was humming a tune she wasn't familiar with, but it was upbeat, and he wiped the saddles to the rhythm.

Chad moved to the other side of the saddles and saw Katrina standing at the end of the barn. "Well, hello there, my wife." Chad beamed with pride. He immediately hungered for her. Katrina's body had changed so much in the last month. Being with child made her even more appetizing to his mind. Some might think him crazy, but he couldn't get enough of her. "Come here, my wife." Chad coaxed Katrina over.

Katrina couldn't help but giggle at him. He never seemed to be sedated anymore. She walked over to him slowly, never losing eye contact with him.

"You are driving me crazy, woman." Chad grabbed her and pulled her into his arms. As he was kissing her, he backed her up against the building. "I want . . . you right . . . now," he said between kisses.

Katrina was excited that Chad wasn't turned off by her body changes. She just hoped as she got further along, he would continue to find her attractive. She felt the baby or babies move again. "Chad, wait." She was pushing him away now."

Chad couldn't think of a time she had ever pushed him away. "What is this? Did you just come out here to tease me?" He was grabbing at her again.

Katrina grabbed his hand. "I want you to feel this." She placed his hand on her rounded belly. She looked at him in awe as she felt the next movement.

Chad couldn't feel anything. "It's too small for me to feel just yet." He sighed with disappointment. "I will be patient, though. In the meantime, where was I?" Chad went to grab at her again, but she stopped him.

"I need to share some news with you."

"Oh! And what might that be?" She had his attention now.

"Well, Mama seems to think, and she is rarely wrong." Katrina paused.

"Go on, woman, do not beat around the bush."

Katrina looked him straight in the eye. This time, she wanted to see his reaction. "Mama believes I am carrying twins."

"Well, of course, you are. Wait! What?" The surprise was amusing for Katrina to watch as it registered on Chad's face. Then came that smile— that sexy smile of his. "Well, I be damned, Katrina. Is there never a dull moment with you?" Chad picked her up and swung her around and around.

"Chad, put me down this instance," Katrina playfully scolded him. Chad did as requested. "Now I have a few minutes before Mama and I have to begin putting together the lunch meal, so if you want to wash up and meet me in our bedroom in ten minutes, I will gladly show you this body you seem to be so in lust over."

Chad couldn't believe his ears. "Ya do not need to ask me twice, woman. I will probably beat you there." Chad smacked her in the rump as she turned to walk away.

A few minutes later, Chad got to the bedroom, and Katrina made good on her promise. She lay totally naked on their bed. Chad locked the door and approached her.

"Look!" She pointed at her belly as she lay on her back. "You might not be able to feel them yet, but you can see them moving. See?" She pointed as her tummy made a little movement again. Katrina was in such awe of the beauty of what she was feeling to have life developing in her.

Chad sat on the side of the bed. His erection forgotten as he watched his babies moving oh so slightly in their mama's tummy. "What does it feel like?" he asked with such wonder.

"It is like a flutter. I find it hard to believe that in just a day, there is so much activity. I wonder if I was feeling a little before and did not know what I was feeling. Today, there is so much going on in there. See?" She pointed again as a bigger movement happened.

"Yes, I see. It is beautiful, Katrina. This is our babies playing together already." Chad smiled at her. "I could sit and watch them play all day."

Katrina took his hand with both of hers and stated in a matter-of-fact voice. "Oh no, you will not. Otherwise, I will call you the tease. I have better things planned for you, mister."

Chad immediately started taking off his clothes. "Again, ya do not have to ask me twice, woman."

A while later, Chad and Katrina walked into the kitchen to see Evelyn working on the lunch meal. "Sorry, Mama. I am here to help now. I got a little tied up." She and Chad blushed and laughed together.

Evelyn looked over at the two of them, so happy and in love. This made her a little lonesome for her late husband, Charles. "I got this taken care of, Katrina. Why not go outside with Chad until I ring the bell? Enjoy the rest of the morning together. Shortly, there will be little time for this kind of romance, so take advantage of it while you can."

Wiser words were never spoken as far as Chad was concerned. He knew they would have plenty of help with little ones around the Holt Ranch once the babies arrived, but he also knew life would never be the same again once they arrived.

Chad grabbed a chair from the front porch and carried it out to the back of the barn where he could continue his chore of oiling the saddles. He set the chair up under the tree so Katrina wouldn't get too much sun.

"Thank you." She smiled at him.

"Now you sit yourself there, and we will talk about baby names," Chad teasingly ordered her.

"Is that right? Did you have anything in mind? Someone you would like to name a son or daughter after?" Katrina asked, holding her breath. She had already been giving the names of a boy or girl some thought. Now they would need two boy names or two girl names or one of each.

"How about you? Is there a name that you like?" Chad had been thinking of different names, but he assumed Katrina would want to pick out the name. Now there were names, as in plural, to be picked out. I figured you would want a boy named after your pa, Charles."

"Well, I thought of that, but I decided to leave that honor to Bo. I think he should be the one to use pa's name down the road."

Chad nodded in agreement. "That is very kind of you to put Bo before yourself." He truly meant it. Trina was one of the most unselfish people he had ever met.

Katrina felt so content in life right now. She could only hope they would always be this happy. "Chad, if we have a son, I would like to name him after you, but with two babies, it would not be fair to a second son born at the same time. What do you think?"

Chad really hadn't had a chance to think about more than one son at a time, up until now. "I rightly do not know how that should work. I guess we need to give it some deep thought. What about a girl's name. What were you thinking?"

"Well, I like Mary, and it would go well with a boy's name of Mark for twins." Katrina was hopeful.

"I like both of those names. Mary and Mark it is. How about if it is two boys, we call them Mark and Mike, and if two girls, Mary and Maggy?"

"It is settled then. I like all those choices." Katrina beamed up at Chad. He couldn't help himself; he had to kiss her again. Chad knelt down and pushed himself between her legs and laid his head on her belly, cherishing this moment with her. Katrina combed her fingers through his hair. "Chad, I love you so much, sometimes it hurts."

Chad looked up at his wife, who seemed to always have tears in her eyes, with his own tears of joy. Katrina wiped the lone tear from his cheek, and he kissed her so tenderly. "May God always bless our family, Katrina."

Epilogue

Katrina sat in bed, holding Chadwick Allen Miles II. This birth had been a breeze. "You, my little man, are the special one. No sharing of the womb for you. How did you get so lucky?" Katrina was kissing his cheek and cooing to him.

Everyone came bursting into the bedroom door, all at once, startling baby Chad, and he began to cry.

His pa took him from his ma's arms to introduce him to all his siblings. "Okay, buddy, these are your three sisters, Mary, Maggy, and Maddie. The triplets, now six, were overly anxious to hold him.

Mary spoke first. "I get to hold him first because I am the oldest," she explained with no argument allowed.

"In a minute, Mary. Chad needs to meet all his siblings first," Katrina berated.

Then turning to the boys, Chad told baby Chad, "And these are your big brothers, Mark and Mike." The twin boys were undecided about their new baby brother.

Mike said, "Put him down to walk now, Pa."

"Oh, he cannot walk for a long time yet, Mike. He is too little," Katrina explained.

"Well, the baby calves and horses walk when they are first born," Mike explained.

Evelyn had walked into the room to hear the conversation and started laughing. Everyone began laughing, except for Mike and Mark. They didn't understand at the age of three why their baby brother couldn't walk yet.

Evelyn ushered the five children out of the room with a promise of cookies and milk as she winked at Katrina. "Get some rest, honey. I will keep them entertained with the help of Tim and Tom.

Katrina smiled as all the noise died down at once. With a heavy sigh, she looked at Chad holding their son. "What do you think of your little namesake, Mr. Miles?"

Chad sat on the edge of the bed. He felt so filled with love. "I do not know how you do it, Trina, but you are amazing. You make such beautiful babies. You hold yourself as a mother and wife so graciously. You are an angel."

"We make beautiful babies, and it is team work. We are all blessed to have you as the head of our household. Thank you for being the wonderful man that you are."

Baby Chad decided he was hungry and began to fuss. Chad looked down at his son and said with jealousy, "I guess I have to share your ma with you son." He then looked at Katrina with hunger in his eyes.

"Chad Miles, you are too much. I just had a baby. You know the drill. You shall have to wait a while."

Chad wiggled his eyebrows at her. "I know, but we still have two bedrooms to fill."

Katrina couldn't believe her ears. "Are you kidding me? There are six bedrooms in this house, and we have six children. By my count, every room is filled and then some."

"No, the triplets take only one room and the twins take only one room and Chad here. He will not want to be in a room alone, so he will want a companion as soon as possible, and then there are still two rooms to fill." Chad was laughing so hard at the looks she was giving him as he totaled up the still-empty rooms.

"Chad Miles, if I was not nursing your son right now, I would throw a pillow at you to knock some sense into that head of yours. How many babies do you want anyway?"

Chad walked over and kissed her forehead then seriously said, "I think I have plenty of blessings, but my biggest is you."

Made in the USA
San Bernardino, CA
28 February 2018